Beli
and

She heard the door slam and then Hal was standing in front of her, staring down at her in the small, feminine room. He looked very male and overpowering.

Slowly he placed his hands on her shoulders. A shock ran through her body and she flinched.

"Why are you afraid of me, Belinda?"

"I—I'm not afraid of you."

"Yes you are. You're quivering like a little cornered mouse."

Oh, yes. The mouse again. The one he was going to pounce on. Not if she had anything to do with it. And she was not really afraid of him—only of what he was capable of doing to her carefully constructed defenses. But she was afraid of the new and unexpected feelings he aroused in her....

KAY GREGORY grew up in England, but moved to Canada as a teenager. She now lives in Vancouver with her husband, two sons, one dog and two ferrets. She has had innumerable jobs, some interesting, some extremely boring, which have often provided background for her books. Now that she is writing romance novels, Kay thinks she has at last found a job that she won't want to leave.

Books by Kay Gregory

HARLEQUIN PRESENTS

1191—NO WAY TO SAY GOODBYE

HARLEQUIN ROMANCE

2919—A STAR FOR A RING
3016—A PERFECT BEAST
3058—IMPULSIVE BUTTERFLY
3082—AMBER AND AMETHYST

KAY GREGORY

the music of love

Harlequin Books

TORONTO • NEW YORK • LONDON
AMSTERDAM • PARIS • SYDNEY • HAMBURG
STOCKHOLM • ATHENS • TOKYO • MILAN

This book is dedicated, with love,
to my friend, Anne Huband,
to her husband, David, who insisted on
'Belinda,' and to all the
Gang at the Steveston Bicycle Shop

Harlequin Presents first edition April 1991
ISBN 0-373-11352-8

Original hardcover edition published in 1990
by Mills & Boon Limited

THE MUSIC OF LOVE

Printed in U.S.A.

CHAPTER ONE

THERE she was again. The girl with the earphones and the dog.

He had been passing her at the same time each day for the past two weeks now, and yet this was the first time Hal could remember feeling even so much as a spark of curiosity about the mouselike little person. Surprising himself, he ran a speculative eye over the small grey figure walking briskly towards him along the trail.

She was older than he had thought, but not more than twenty-five or six. And that was odd, because if anyone had asked him before he would have said she was scarcely more than a child. But then he hadn't really looked at her before, had he? Shapeless little women in baggy jogging-suits, out walking their dogs, were not the sort of scenery calculated to rivet his attention at six o'clock on a chilly April morning in the middle of his daily run.

No, he thought, but on the other hand if our paths are fated to cross at this ridiculous hour every day, sooner or later it will be necessary to acknowledge each other's existence.

Might as well be sooner, he decided, slowing his pace and opening his mouth to offer a polite 'good morning'. Then he closed it again. Of course, they wouldn't be able to hear each other, would they? She was wearing earphones. So was he. Idly he wondered if they could both be listening to Hank Williams, then almost immediately he was willing to bet they weren't.

But the girl had noticed his half-hearted attempt to speak, and now she too slowed her steps. Hal saw the awkward beginnings of a smile on her soft, upturned lips, and then, when he didn't respond at once, the beginnings of a delicate blush.

The colour suited her, he noted. She didn't look nearly so grey and unobtrusive any more. And maybe there *was* a figure under that hopeless sweatshirt after all.

He raised a muscular arm in salute and gave her a broad, inviting smile.

The girl's pale white skin turned from pink to fiery red. She made a quick motion to the odd-shaped dog, ordering it to remove its nose from something green and mouldering beneath the trees, and then averted her head to hurry stiffly past him around a bend in the path.

The next morning Hal jogged the entire length of the trail and back again—twice, instead of his usual once. But for the first time in two weeks there was no sign of the small, grey-clad woman or of her black apology for a dog.

'It's not fair, Misty,' muttered Belinda. 'You and I have been taking that trail through the park for years. And now we have to walk on the road, or else go at a different time of day.'

The little black dog thumped its sideways question-mark tail and looked anxious.

'I know. You think I'm stupid, don't you?' Belinda sighed and spun the wheel of the bicycle which was upturned on her kitchen floor. 'You're probably right. I am being stupid. And it was fine as long as that handsome man ignored us. But now that he's condescended to notice me, I just don't feel comfortable any more. He's so—so intimidatingly good-looking.' She shrugged and turned back to the bike. 'Of course that *shouldn't* make any difference, should it? I'm not usually in the habit of going all silly and self-conscious over some gorgeous hunk's come-hither smile.'

Misty wagged her tail again, with less conviction, and put her soft, seal-like face on Belinda's knee.

'It doesn't make sense, does it?' She stroked the dog's head absently. 'Men *don't* notice me. And that's exactly the way I like it.'

She twisted the wrench in her hand defiantly, and promptly broke the spoke she was attempting to tighten.

'Mmph,' snurfed Misty. She slid her head encouragingly up her mistress's leg as Belinda crouched on a stool beside the bike and glared at the mutilated wheel.

'Oh, you're a big help,' she grumbled. 'Now the damn thing's broken—just because I didn't get the tension right, I suppose.' She sighed heavily. 'I wonder whether it *was* me. It could have been a faulty spoke.'

'It was you, girl,' said a gruff voice behind her. 'I know you can fix most things, but straightening a warped wheel is a job for someone who knows what he's doing.'

'Hello, Joe. Yes, I expect it is.' Belinda wiped her hands on her track-suit and stood up. 'It's just that I'd rather do it myself if I can.'

'I know you would. Too independent by half, that's your trouble. Well, *I* can't fix it for you, girl, so you'll just have to take it into Blake's.'

'To Nanaimo? Yes, I suppose I will.'

'Nope.' Joe ran a gnarled hand over his full white beard and plumped himself down on a chair beside the table. 'Don't have to go all the way to Nanaimo any more. Blake's have opened a bike shop here in Cinnamon Bay.'

'Have they?' Belinda's pert little face registered relief, and her short dark curls bounced on her neck as she lifted two cups from the yellow-painted cupboard. 'Well, that is good news. I'll load this contraption in the truck tomorrow then and run it over to them.'

Joe eyed her sourly. 'If you didn't hide yourself back here in the bush all the time, my girl, you'd know what was new in this town.'

'I *don't* hide myself, Joe. I've just been busy lately. I've had a lot of animals to look after because everyone's away for Easter.'

'Huh. I know, so you've been nipping down the highway for your groceries, and you haven't seen a soul in weeks. You and your animals.'

Belinda laughed and handed him a cup of coffee. 'I *like* looking after animals, Joe, and along with what Dad left me, it gives me enough to live on. Besides, I see people all the time—when they come with their cats and dogs.'

'Huh,' grunted Joe again. 'Not to mention rats, snakes, birds, ferrets, frogs, mice . . .'

'Yes, but I enjoy them,' interrupted Belinda. 'Anyway, you're a fine one to talk. You hide yourself down the lane with your canvases and oils, and half the time you only see me.'

'Different. I'm old. And when I'm painting I don't *want* to see anyone. I only see you because you're my neighbour. And *you* don't know enough to stay away.'

Belinda shook her head. 'You're an ungrateful old curmudgeon, Joe,' she reproved him affectionately.

Joe grinned suddenly, a surprising, gap-toothed grin.

'If I'm a curmudgeon, then you're a stubborn little donkey, Bella. You going to take that bike in like I said?'

'Yes, I told you I was. Why?'

'No reason. Never know when you might need it, though. Truck's on its last legs.'

'No, it isn't, Joe. I've just had it serviced.' Belinda stared at him, puzzled.

'Hmm. All the same, you take the bike in. You hear me?'

Yes, thought Belinda after he had left. I heard you all right. How could I avoid it?

Old Joe, with his fuss about her bike, seemed to be going rapidly round the bend. He had never shown the smallest interest in her transportation before.

But the next day, when she unloaded the bike from her pick-up truck and pushed open the door of Blake's shiny new bicycle shop, she began to have an inkling of the reason behind Joe's sudden concern. He had been insisting for years that she ought to meet more young men. And the man in the jeans and blue denim shirt with his back to her was undoubtedly young.

When he lowered his hands from the bicycle he was working on and turned to face her, she saw that he was also the nemesis of her early-morning walks.

Belinda swallowed. He might be dressed in working clothes, but somehow that only added to the air of powerful masculinity he exuded. And he was tall, but not so tall that there was any reason for her to feel so physically overwhelmed that she had to conquer an urge to turn around and run.

In an effort to do something about this ridiculous assault on her senses, she looked away from the penetrating, almost-black eyes, and gazed desperately at the walls of the shop.

On two sides she was fenced in by racks of bicycles of every conceivable shape and size, all very bright and new. A few more bikes were suspended from the ceiling, but several shelves and a peg-board, presumably intended for tools and accessories, were almost empty. Obviously the shop had only been open a very short time, although from the indignantly raised voices she could hear squabbling in the back room, it was apparent that it was fully staffed.

It was also apparent that the incredible man in front of her was very much the boss. As she tried not to stare at him, he turned and shouted over his shoulder to the bickering employees that if they wanted to keep on working for him they could all stop complaining and damn well get on with their jobs.

Belinda ran her tongue over her lips, and immediately he apologised for his bad manners. But the apology was extended so casually that she had the impression it was only a sop to customer relations and that he didn't really believe she had anything to excuse.

'It's all right,' she murmured. And then, almost to herself, she added, 'I might have known.'

Once again she was conscious of his virility as heavy eyelids lifted, and she found herself transfixed by startlingly deep eyes which were only partly shielded by thick, dark lashes. The eyes were studying her intently and with an expression of wary amusement.

'What might you have known?' he asked, and his voice was so low and warm and caressing that Belinda knew she was going to blush—again.

She turned her face away, furious with herself, with him, and with old Joe MacIlwain who—as she *might* have known—had had ulterior motives for insisting that she come here.

After a while she was only furious with Joe.

It wasn't this devastating man's fault that she had come into his shop, and he could hardly be blamed because his overpowering presence had an annoying effect on her complexion.

She became conscious that he had asked a question and was waiting for an answer.

'Nothing,' she mumbled stupidly.

'I see.' He was smiling at her, and his smile was as attractive as the rest of him. He had nice lips—full and strong and made for smiling—or for . . .

Oh, no. No, no, *no*. Since the day of her high-school graduation she had refused to allow herself the luxury of thoughts like that, and she was certainly not going to change her rules now.

'My bike needs repairing,' she said quickly. 'I seem to have broken a spoke.'

'*Seem* to have?' He raised two arched, black eyebrows, and for a moment Belinda wondered if he was being deliberately obtuse. Then she saw that the dark eyes were gleaming at her with a provocation that was certainly deliberate, and she realised he was only poking fun.

Damn the man, she thought indignantly. He's just one of Blake's managers. It's his job to look after bikes, not bait the customers. And just because he has glossy dark hair that waves back nicely from his temples, a disgustingly healthy tan, a tough, square jawline and that improbably heroic figure, he needn't think he has a right to play games with me—just because I'm a woman who happens to have broken a spoke.

'Yes,' she said aggressively. 'It's broken and it needs fixing. So if you'd just do the job and let me know when it's ready . . .'

The dark face before her stopped smiling and Belinda found herself on the receiving end of a very long, contemplative stare. That was when she noticed the lines at the corners of his eyes. Lines which indicated there had been shadows in this man's life that had not been quite so obvious on her first awestruck appraisal.

'I do believe the mouse has roared,' she heard him say approvingly, as she brought her mind firmly back to the here and now. 'So much for my preconceptions.'

'And just what do you mean by *that*?' Belinda, unable to believe this conversation was happening, realised she was fighting a most unusual urge to shout. To make matters worse, this maddeningly impressive specimen of manhood was raising his arm so that all the muscles tightened across his chest as he ran a hand through his thick, waving hair. Belinda wondered if he was aware of what a mouth-watering picture he presented. Then she decided he couldn't be, because the casual gesture had just transferred a wide smear of bike grease from his large hand to the now partially flattened hair.

'Damn,' he exploded, as it dawned on him what he had done. And then, as Belinda stared at him, unsure whether to laugh or beat a hasty retreat from the shop, 'Do you realise this is all your fault?'

'No,' said Belinda, for the first time feeling she had the upper hand. 'It's entirely your own fault. And now if you'd just fill out a receipt for my bike I'll be going. Then *you* can go and wash your hair.'

The light of retaliation flared in his eyes and he took a quick step forward. For a moment when he lifted his hand, Belinda thought he meant to hit her. Then she saw that he only wanted to check her bike. He made a cursory examination of the wheel that had caused all the trouble, then shouldered the bicycle and carried it to the rear of the shop. In a moment he was back and standing behind the counter.

'Right,' he said, his voice all brusque business again. 'It should be ready on Thursday, Miss . . .' He raised his eyebrows and paused with his pen poised on a pad of receipts.

'Ballantyne,' she said. 'Belinda Ballantyne.'

'Good grief.' He looked up, startled. 'Are you serious?'

'Shouldn't I be?'

He shrugged. 'I suppose there's no reason why not.'

'I know,' she said drily. 'It makes me sound like a movie star, doesn't it? And you don't think I fit the image?'

'That's not what I said, Miss Ballantyne.'

'No, but I seem to remember you *did* call me a mouse with a roar. You can't have it both ways, Mr . . .' She raised her own dark eyebrows in a deliberate imitation of his.

And at that the surprising man behind the counter signed his name boldly, ripped the receipt off the pad and handed it to her with a grin.

'Blake,' he said, tapping his signature with the pen. 'Hal Blake. At your service.'

Belinda gaped at him 'Blake,' she repeated. 'You mean you're *the* Hal Blake?'

A half-smile tugged at the corner of his mouth. '*The* Hal Blake? How very flattering. I'd no idea my fame had travelled so far.'

He really was terribly attractive when he smiled. 'Well, you're not exactly on a par with Prince Charles or Paul McCartney,' said Belinda dampeningly, 'but your bike shops *are* all over Vancouver Island, not to mention the rest of British Columbia. And everyone knows about your donations to kids' sports teams and . . . oh, all those charitable things.'

'Definitely flattering,' he murmured. 'Keep it up, and I might even have your bike ready for you by Wednesday.'

Belinda didn't answer, because he was looking at her in that amused, appraising way again, and suddenly she didn't know where to put her eyes. So she nodded, turned her back on him and, feeling gauche and embarrassingly foolish, almost scuttled out of the shop.

Behind her, to her chagrin, she heard a low, very sexy chuckle.

'Oh, Misty,' she moaned a short time later, as she pulled the truck to a jerking stop beneath the trees and the little dog ran to meet her. 'Oh, Misty, I've just made a complete idiot of myself. And I honestly don't understand why.'

She didn't either. Ever since she had been a teenager, she had avoided the opposite sex, other than on a strictly casual or business basis, and she had never gone through the normal moonstruck, movie-star pin-up stage. So why had her reaction to Hal Brake, from the moment she had first seen him running in the park, been precisely that moonstruck, tongue-tied admiration she had read about, but never expected to experience for herself? It *didn't* make sense. Nor did that ridiculous scene in the bike shop. In fact it didn't make sense that Hal was even there, repairing bicycles like any ordinary mechanic, when everyone knew he owned upwards of twenty very successful stores, all of which were run by competent managers while the great man himself sat back and organised his profits.

Belinda stroked Misty's head thoughtfully. Yes, everyone knew it all right. But then maybe everyone was wrong.

Irrelevantly, she pictured him now, bent over a sink at the back of his shop as he washed the grease from his hair. An unusual but intriguing vision of the great Hal Blake. She was grinning to herself as, with Misty at her side, she made her way into the cottage's small kitchen. Then she remembered his face at the moment when he had made that unwary swipe at his head and realised, too late, what he had done . . .

Her grin broadened. Oh, handsome Hal might think he was the king of the castle, and amuse himself by poking fun at unsophisticated little women from the country—but he had proved he could also be quite satisfactorily human.

Anyway, she needn't concern herself with him any more because on Thursday she would ask Joe to collect her bike for her. She sighed, and shook her head resignedly at Misty. It was all very well that Joe could pick up the bike, but from now on her early morning walks could not be early.

For a moment she wondered if she was being a coward, but then she decided there was nothing particularly reprehensible about preferring to exercise her dog without the uncomfortable probability of meeting a man she would rather avoid.

Funny, when they had met again in the bike shop neither of them had even mentioned those early encounters in the park when they had both blocked the world out with earphones. Unless you counted Hal Blake's enigmatic reference to preconceptions.

Hal swung Belinda's well-used bicycle down from the repair stand, glanced at his watch which read six p.m. and shouted, 'Jerry!'

A thin, ginger-haired boy with freckles poked his head round the door to the back of the shop. 'Is it time to go home, Dad?' he asked doubtfully. 'I thought you said you might be working late.'

'It is late. Everyone's already gone,' replied Hal. When Jerry continued to eye him disapprovingly he turned his head away and added curtly, 'Besides, we're almost caught up, and I want to drop off this bike on our way home.'

Jerry looked even more dubious. 'You mean we're making deliveries now, Dad?' He frowned. 'Grandma always says you don't know how to relax, but . . .'

Hal gave a short, derisive snort and ran an affectionate hand through Jerry's tousled hair. 'That doesn't sound like Grandma. What did she really say?'

Jerry jerked his head away and edged towards the door of the shop.

'She said you've had ants in your pants ever since the day you learned to walk—and that you'll drive her to an early grave.'

'Disrespectful brat,' said Hal, taking a threatening step towards his son.

'Well, you did ask,' Jerry pointed out aggrievedly.

'True. And I've no doubt Grandma said exactly that. One of these days I'll have to stop letting you stay with her.'

'You won't though. She says if she couldn't have me with her in Victoria during term-time, then you wouldn't be able to charge round the province opening up new stores and stirring up old managers, and . . .'

'Grandma says a great deal too much. Come on, wheel this bike outside. I'm going to start the truck.'

'Why *are* we delivering that beat-up old heap?' asked Jerry a few minutes later, as they sped down the highway in a newly painted white truck emblazoned in large letters with the words Blake's Bicycle Shop.

Hal smiled, a long, speculative smile. 'Mainly so I can play cat to a certain mouse who has aroused my interest,' he said cryptically. 'I feel in the mood to pounce.'

Jerry stared at him, shook his head disgustedly and gave up.

But when the truck pulled to a screeching stop in front of a small cedar shake cottage among the trees, Hal discovered that his hunting trip was in vain, because the mouse he had planned to pounce on was not in her nest.

After pounding on the door with a blatant disregard for the eardrums of anyone who might be inside, and receiving no response beyond a cacophony of frantic barking, he returned to the truck and lifted the bike to the ground.

'What are you doing, Dad?' enquired Jerry.

'There's no sign of rain, so I'm leaving the heap round the back.'

'But the lady won't know it's there.'

'Yes, she will. I'll phone her.'

'But what if . . .'

'Jerry, contrary to current youthful wisdom, thirty-five-year-old fathers do occasionally know what they're doing. If you were going to tell me the lady might be on holiday, she's not.'

'Oh.'

Hal watched his son weigh the compulsion to ask how he knew, against the probability that the question would provoke a sharp order to mind his own business. When he judged that Jerry was about to burst with the strain of making a decision, he took pity and explained that Mrs Barclay at the café had told him Miss

Ballantyne never left her cottage unattended for more than a very short time because she had to look after her animals.

'Animals?' said Jerry brightening. 'Maybe we *should* wait until she comes back.'

'No,' said Hal firmly. 'We shouldn't.'

His mild interest in the strange young woman with the pale complexion, turned up nose and enormous pansy-flower eyes did not extend to standing around a wooded clearing on a cool April evening while hunger pangs gnawed at his insides. The prospect of a hot meal was infinitely more attractive.

With the dogs still challenging them eagerly, he and Jerry climbed back into the truck.

As they pulled away, Hal reflected that there were advantages to living in a small town which he had never considered before. If it hadn't been for the enthusiastic gossip of the café's garrulous Mrs Barclay, he would never have known that Belinda was unlikely to go away. Nor would he have known that she was considered a quiet little thing who kept herself to herself. Or that she had lived in the cottage on the outskirts of Cinnamon Bay since she was only two years old. That was when her father had brought her to live there after his marriage broke up. If it had been a marriage. Mrs Barclay said no one seemed sure about that. In any case Steven Ballantyne, who had made a reasonable living writing books about wilderness survival, had died five years ago leaving everything to his daughter—who had promptly started up a boarding-house for pets. As a lot of Cinnamon Bay's residents were retired, and had unlimited time to travel, Belinda's business was reputed to be doing quite well.

Hall was still thinking of the young woman with the

glamorous name and the much less glamorous appearance as he swung the truck briskly round a bend in the lane and almost ran her over.

CHAPTER TWO

'ARE you all right?' shouted Hal. He jumped down from the cab and strode over to Belinda, who was struggling to disentangle herself from the clutches of a wild blackberry bush in which she had landed when she leaped from his path.

'No,' said Belinda, glaring at him. 'I am *not* all right. Nor would you be if you'd just been turned into a pincushion because some hulking great idiot didn't look where he was going.' She squirmed sideways, lodged herself more securely in the bush, and winced.

Hal passed a hand across his mouth. 'From *the* Hal Blake to hulking great idiot at a stroke,' he murmured. 'How deflating.'

'It's me that's deflating,' moaned Belinda. 'I feel like a pricked balloon. Help me out of here, for heaven's sake, don't just stand there laughing.'

'I'm not laughing.' Hal extended both hands, gripped her beneath the arms and pulled her clear. For a moment her body was pinned against his chest, and she glanced up at him, startled by a sensation quite new to her. An odd, breathless feeling that seemed to ripple back and forth inside her. Then his hands moved, and brushed briefly over her breasts before they fell back at his sides.

'Thank you,' said Belinda stiffly, and from the ice in her voice Hal suspected that her thanks were as barbed as the thorns she was picking out of her fingers.

'Any time. And I'm sorry. I didn't see you.'

'I didn't imagine you had,' she replied drily. 'Not unless running people over is a hobby.'

Hal stared at her, but resisted the urge to tell her not to be smart. After all, her present prickly condition was entirely his fault. 'No, it's not a hobby,' he told her evenly. 'Can I drive you home?'

'No, thank you. I'm looking for Misty—my dog. She's missing.'

'Can I help?'

'You've done enough, thanks.'

Hal's lip curled. 'Your current resemblance to a porcupine seems appropriate,' he remarked. 'Are you always this easy to get along with?'

'Only when I'm almost run over. Are you always so rude?'

He grinned suddenly. 'Only when I know I'm in the wrong. Forgive me.'

His dark eyes were gleaming so outrageously and the grin was so impossibly seductive that for a moment Belinda would have forgiven, or given, him anything.

Then she saw something move on the other side of the truck, and at once she forgot about Hal and ran quickly across the lane.

Seated on a mossy bank beneath the trees, she saw a ginger-haired boy of about twelve. Beside him, Misty was stretched out with her head on his lap. Her brown eyes gazed up at him adoringly and her long tail was drumming out a beat on the ground. It was the thumping, question-mark tail that had drawn her attention.

'Hi,' said Belinda in surprise. 'Where did you spring from?'

'From my Dad's truck. Didn't you see me?'

'No, I was busy having an argument with a bush.'

'I know, I saw you. You looked funny. Then I saw the dog. Is she yours?'

'Yes, her name's Misty.'

'Hi, Misty.' Jerry scratched the dog's ear, and she gave an approving little snurf and wriggled closer.

Belinda became conscious that Hal was standing close behind her.

'If you're sure I can't do anything to make amends, we'd better be on our way,' he told her. 'By the way, I left your bike at the back of the cottage.'

'Oh. Thank you. Is that what you're doing out this way? I didn't know you delivered.'

'We don't,' said Jerry.

Hal glared at him. 'In certain cases we do.'

Belinda saw something flare between the tall man and his son—and she wondered. 'Well, it's very nice of you,' she said quickly. 'How did you know where I lived?'

'Mrs Barclay.'

For the first time since she had landed in the blackberries, Belinda laughed. 'Of course. Why did I even ask?'

'Why indeed?' Hal's eyes met hers in perfect understanding. Then he said, 'Come on, Jerry,' and jerked his head peremptorily at the truck. Reluctantly, Jerry patted Misty and stood up.

Something in the cheeky, freckled face touched Belinda, some echo or memory of her own often lonely childhood, and on an impulse she said, 'If you'd like to see Misty again, Jerry, you're welcome to come over.'

'Gee, thanks.' Jerry beamed. 'Can I, Dad?'

'I don't see why not.' The deep voice was very low, and it seemed to curl softly around her like a warm, enfolding blanket. Belinda closed her eyes for a moment, wishing with an odd sort of panic that she hadn't issued that impulsive invitation to Jerry. Then, seeing his cheerful face, she was glad she had.

Ten minutes later, watched by Misty and three visiting dogs, she was back in her snug, warm kitchen, busy with a needle and tweezers as she plucked countless tiny barbs from beneath her skin.

Now, at last, when she no longer felt the need to put on a careless front for Hal's benefit, she could say 'ouch' without reservation. But, in spite of the discomfort, she found that she was smiling. That frustratingly attractive man hadn't been far off the mark when he'd accused her of resembling a porcupine. Only she had an uncomfortable feeling he had been referring to her disposition, not the current condition of her skin.

She shrugged, and remarked firmly to the dogs that it made no difference anyway, because she wasn't going to see him again, was she? When she received Blake's bill for the bicycle, she could easily send the money. And even if Jerry did come over to see Misty, he was almost certain to come alone.

She was right. He did come alone, two days later when she had just finished settling in a new pet. He said he had walked the two and a half miles from town, so Belinda gave him lunch, and in the end he stayed for the whole afternoon. Most of the time he played in the back with the dogs. She was just on the point of suggesting he had better go home before dark when the woodland peace was shattered by an agonised yell. Within seconds Misty slid into the cottage on the run, whining anxiously.

'What is it?' asked Belinda, hurrying to the door as the little dog darted back and forth across the floor.

But the moment she reached the lawn and saw the thin figure sitting on the grass prodding gingerly at his ankle, she was sure she knew exactly what had happened, and her heart dropped leadenly into her toes.

Obviously Jerry had caught his foot in one of the many potholes dug by enthusiastic dogs in pursuit of mythical moles or rabbits. The only question to be answered now was regarding the extent of the damage.

'Is it broken?' she asked, kneeling down beside him.

'I don't know. But it hurts.'

'All right, hang on a minute while I put the dogs back in the kennels. Then we'll see if you can walk.'

She rounded up two doubtful mongrels and a beautiful, silky spaniel and shepherded them into a shed that was built against the back of her cottage. When she returned to Jerry, his face had gone an interesting shade of green.

'Come on,' she said, putting an arm beneath his shoulders. 'Let's try and get you inside.'

With much pulling and tugging, and with Jerry's face going greener by the minute, she finally managed to haul him to his feet. But when he touched his right foot to the ground, although he could still hobble, it was certain that he would not be walking home.

'I think it's just a sprain,' she told him, after he had hopped his way into the house and flopped down on her blue and white flowered sofa in front of the unlit fireplace.

'Oh,' said Jerry, looking crestfallen. 'Does that mean I'll be able to go to school?'

Belinda laughed. 'I shouldn't think so. Not for a few days anyway. But school doesn't start again till Monday, does it?'

'No, but I was supposed to go back to Victoria tomorrow. I stay with my Grandma during term-time.'

'Oh,' said Belinda, surprised. 'But couldn't you go to school here?'

'I might next year if Dad stays long enough. Usually

he doesn't.'

'He doesn't?' She frowned. 'Jerry, what on earth do you mean?'

Jerry shrugged. 'Well, he started with just the big store in Victoria, but now he has shops all over the province. So he travels round visiting them—upsetting them, Grandma says—and about every six months he opens up a new one. Then when the holidays come I go to stay with him wherever he happens to be.'

Belinda heard the wistful note in his voice which he was trying so hard to conceal, and she felt a pang of sympathy for the motherless boy—who would soon be a motherless teenager. That was when trouble would start, she thought, with a surprising stab of resentment at Jerry's foot-loose father.

It was only much later that it occurred to her to wonder what had happened to Hal's wife.

Now all she said was, 'I see. How lucky you've got your grandma.'

'Mm, but *she's* mad at Dad all the time. She says he ought to buy a house and settle down, instead of flying all over B.C.'

'But he does have to run his business,' objected Belinda.

'Grandma says his managers get along fine when he leaves them alone, and that he ought to run the business from Victoria.'

'Oh.' Belinda decided that this discussion of what was definitely not her concern had gone on quite long enough. And deep down she knew that she had only let it go this far because she was reluctant to make the phone call that she knew could not be put off for much longer.

'I like your pictures,' commented Jerry, relieving her

of the necessity to change the subject.

'Pictures?'

'On the wall. Dogs and cats . . .'

'And beavers and bears,' smiled Belinda. 'Yes, I like them too.' She took a determined breath and added loudly, 'OK, Jerry. I think it's time I phoned your father. He'll have to pick you up because I can't leave the animals for long and I don't think my neighbour is available to dog-sit at the moment.'

Jerry, whose face had returned to its normal colour, grinned and replied cheerfully, 'Dad won't mind much. I expect he's still waiting to pounce.'

'What?' Belinda gaped at him. 'What are you talking about, Jerry?'

'Dad. When we delivered your bike the other day he said he wanted to play cat and mouse. With you, I think. Anyway he's always pouncing. Grandma gets mad about that too. She says it's time he stopped seeing women as conveniences with long legs and sexy . . .'

'OK, Jerry,' said Belinda hastily. 'I get the picture. Just give me a minute to phone.'

She bit her lip and hurried into the kitchen. Cat and mouse! Of all the nerve. And if Jerry was right, and Hal Blake really had planned to pounce in her direction, the pickings in Cinnamon Bay must be slim indeed. Her legs were not long, no part of her was long, and as for sexy . . . well, she'd given up all ambitions in that line on the night of her graduation.

Belinda was muttering out loud by the time she picked up the phone, and she was wishing she could give both adult Blakes, mother and son, a strong piece of her mind about what she thought of people who discussed intimate personal matters in front of children.

If anyone knew about that sort of thing she did.

'Blake's Bicycles.' Hal's voice snapped across the wires, and Belinda wondered how he ever did any business if that was the tone he normally took with customers.

'It's Belinda Ballantyne,' she began coldly.

'Oh. Miss Ballantyne. Listen, I'll call you back . . .'

'No, you won't,' she said quickly. 'I've got Jerry, and I think he's sprained his ankle.'

Hal's breath was expelled on a long sigh of relief. 'Thank heaven for that,' he said shortly, and Belinda wished she could pour a fresh layer of bike grease on his hair. Really, he was an exceptionally rude man, and if he had been worried about Jerry, that was *his* fault, not hers. He should have kept a sharper eye on his son.

'If you're thanking heaven because Jerry has sprained his ankle, you're a very odd sort of parent,' she told him bluntly.

'Don't be an idiot. He said he'd be back two hours ago, and I was worried because the friend he was visiting told me he left his house at twelve o'clock. Anyway, don't worry. I'll be over right away.' Without waiting for an answer, he hung up the phone in her ear.

Don't be an idiot. Don't worry! Did he really think she was incapable of coping on her own? Belinda was frowning to herself as she mixed a large cup of cocoa for Jerry, and, by the time Hal arrived a few minutes later, the frown had become a full-fledged scowl.

He took one look at her face, nodded complacently, and said, 'Porcupine. I knew those spikes were appropriate.'

Belinda stared up at him, very cool and collected, and resisted a strong inclination to kick him sharply on the shins. 'According to Jerry you were hoping I'd be a mouse. Do you think we could forget these woodland comparisons for the moment and get on with seeing to your son?'

'Ouch.' Hal winced. 'We'll certainly forget the mouse. My son has an unfortunate habit of putting my foot in his mouth. As for the porcupine—is it possible to get past the quills?' He was still lounging in the doorway, but now he slammed it behind him and took a step into the room. He was standing much too close, very male and overpowering, and she could smell the scent of his soap in the soft April dusk. 'No,' she said, moving swiftly backwards. 'It isn't possible.' She didn't look at his face as she hurried away from him into the living-room to lead him over to Jerry, who was lying back on the cushions doing a creditable imitation of a wounded hero.

'What's this?' asked Hal sternly, staring down at him. 'I thought you were over at Billy's.'

'I was, but he wanted to go down to the beach and I didn't, so I came over here instead.'

'Why didn't you tell me?'

'I forgot.'

'The world's most over-used excuse,' Hal murmured.

'I expect you used it too.' Belinda found herself jumping to Jerry's defence.

'Of course I did. Only I never got away with it.'

'Jerry hasn't got away with it either. His ankle's sprained.'

'Hmm.' Hal sank down on his heels and moved firm fingers deftly over Jerry's swollen leg. 'Yes, it's a sprain all right. I'll take him to the doctor's just to make sure, though. Tomorrow. Nice going, Jerry. You'll probably miss some school.'

Belinda gazed down at the top of Hal's dark head, lost in reluctant admiration of the way his hair curled on his neck. Then she said slowly, almost unwillingly, 'You'll be in your shop though, won't you? Can I take him to the doctor for you?'

When Hal swivelled round to look up at her the expression on his face was confusing. It was a hard face most of the time, but for once it looked surprisingly gentle. 'Thank you,' he said quietly. 'That's nice of you. But I started a new manager a few days ago. He's learned enough to take over for a couple of hours.'

So he had a new manager—who had learned enough to take over. According to Jerry that probably meant he would be leaving Cinnamon Bay in the near future. The boy had assured her that his father didn't usually stay anywhere for long. Belinda, staring at his bent head, was stunned by a wave of disappointment that almost knocked her off her feet. And she knew that the feeling of weightlessness was caused as much by surprise that she cared where Hal Blake went as it was by the feeling itself. Then she put the whole thing down to the fact that she hadn't eaten yet, and said that in that case she knew Jerry would be in safe hands.

'I'm glad you think so.' Hal stood up, and once again Belinda was conscious of the size and strength of him as he towered above her. The weightless feeling was becoming impossible to control.

'Have—have you eaten?' she asked, with a stifled sort of gasp in her voice.

'Not yet.'

'Oh. Can I—would you like me to fix up something then—for you and Jerry? I haven't eaten either.'

He smiled down at her, a slow, curving smile that curdled her stomach—and immediately she regretted the invitation.

But it was too late.

'If it wouldn't be too much trouble. I do get bored with my own cooking.'

Belinda nodded and turned quickly away from him. 'Mine's not exciting either. There's very little inspiration about cooking just for oneself.'

To her amazement, she felt his hand touch the back of her neck. Then his voice said softly, 'Always for yourself, Belinda? Never for somebody else?'

'Not often. Sometimes Joe next door comes.' She jerked her head away, because his fingers were still on her neck. Moving towards the kitchen, she asked hesitantly, 'Do you cook for yourself too, Mr Blake?'

'Not always. And it's Hal.' She heard the amusement in his tone and was furious with herself for asking. Of course he didn't always cook for himself. He could afford all the housekeeping and catering services he wanted. And all those leggy ladies Jerry had talked about—they must entertain him sometimes—probably in more ways than one.

'I'll get on with it, then,' she said curtly. 'You must want to talk to Jerry.'

She scurried into the kitchen like the mouse he was reputed to have called her—and behind her she heard his low voice murmur with a faint note of malice, 'Do I have a choice, Belinda? Or has the porcupine spoken?'

Damn him, she thought, as she slammed a pan on to the stove and began to grope around in the depths of her small freezer. Why did he have to come into her life now to disrupt all the careful defences she had spent so many years erecting? On the night of her graduation she had vowed never to allow a man to touch her heart or mind—let alone her body—and up until Hal Blake she had succeeded very well. It hadn't been all that difficult either. As she had remarked to Misty that first time Hal had noticed her, men had never been inclined to come clamouring at her door. She wasn't the type. And once she had made up her mind that she was immune to masculine charms, it had not been hard to avoid situations in which her feelings might stand a chance of becoming engaged.

Irritably she pushed aside several packages labelled 'single portion' and lifted out a medium-sized tourtiere. She always made several at a time and she had been saving this French-Canadian meat pie for the next time Joe came over. Well, Joe was out of luck. That disturbing man in the other room would probably eat the whole thing—with a little help from his son.

As she heated the oven she wondered, not for the first time, why this man, of all men, should be having such an unsettling effect on her. He was an impressive specimen of manhood, certainly, but she had never succumbed to appearances before. There must be more to it. But that made no sense either because, from what she had seen of him, he was self-assured and arrogant, not the sort of person she even liked—let alone lusted after.

That brought her up short. *Was* she lusting after him? Belinda gave a small sigh and Misty pricked up her ears. It was possible, of course. But she knew better than to give in to those feelings. Even if Jerry proved right, and Hal did have designs on her, they would be entirely temporary designs—just passing the time—and she didn't need disruptions like that.

As she was setting the table she recalled that her father had told her she shouldn't want permanence either. Dangerous pieces of paper was the way he had referred to marriage lines. Belinda smiled grimly.

She was just testing the tourtiere with her fingers

when the door opened and Hal strolled in with his hands in the pockets of his jeans. As usual he looked quite devastatingly male.

'What's all this Jerry tells me about snakes?' he asked, eyeing her suspiciously.

'Snakes?' Belinda straightened, her face flushed, this time from the heat of the oven.

'Mm. He says you charm them. He always did have a vivid imagination. Not,' he added hastily, 'that I doubt your ability to charm, Belinda. That's assuming you've ever made the effort.'

Belinda glared at him. 'Are you trying to flatter me or insult me, Mr Blake? Either way, your supper's in jeopardy, so I'd suggest you watch it.'

Hal pushed his hands further into his pockets and leaned back comfortably against the wall. 'My name's Hal. And what should I watch?' The smile on his full lips was sheer provocation as his eyes ran thoughtfully over her body in a way that added flame to her already rosy cheeks.

'Your tongue,' said Belinda through clenched teeth. 'That's if you hope to eat.'

Hal lifted his head and sniffed appreciatively. 'If it tastes as good as it smells, I definitely hope to eat. Does the ban on my tongue include snakes?'

'Snake,' said Belinda succinctly, as she chopped up cucumber and green pepper.

'All right, snake. What about it?'

'I've just booked in a boa constrictor for the week.'

'You're not serious?' Hal raised his eyebrows and gave an exaggerated shudder.

'Of course I am.'

'Good lord. And I let my son make your acquaintance. I should have known better.'

'Don't be ridiculous,' snapped Belinda, whose patience was wearing wafer thin. 'Boas aren't dangerous. This one's only five feet long, and he ate before he came.'

'How comforting. I don't think I'll ask what he ate.'

'I shouldn't. Not if you're squeamish.'

'I gather you're not.'

'Well, I couldn't feed him anything live,' admitted Belinda, 'but apart from that I rather like snakes.'

'You're an amazing woman, Belinda Ballantyne. I can't stand them.'

'Really?' She was surprised.

'Really. I'd be no good at all as one of those movie marvels who spend their time rescuing beautiful redheads from slithery things in the jungle.'

'How disillusioning,' murmured Belinda, feeling rather pleased that there was something he wasn't bursting with confidence about.

Her back was to him as she bent over the table, and now she jumped as she felt his hand on her shoulder. 'Did you have illusions then, Belinda?' His voice was very deep and soft.

'No,' she said, wriggling away from his fingers. 'Of course not.'

Behind her she heard a long, lugubrious sigh. 'I was afraid you hadn't.'

She was spared the necessity of answering, because at that moment Jerry called from the other room, and Hal went to see what was the matter.

As it turned out, nothing was, although Jerry insisted that he was suffering from a case of advanced starvation. Hal, telling his son he ought to be grateful to Belinda and not to be such a damned little pest, carried him into the kitchen and propped his foot on a stool. A short time later the three of them sat down at the polished pine table to eat.

'This is great,' enthused Jerry, as he accepted a second helping. 'Usually I don't like food I haven't eaten before.'

'And isn't that the truth,' murmured Hal, rolling his eyes at the ceiling. 'Jerry's right though. This is terrific.'

Belinda smiled, pleased, and at the same time startled at the extent of her pleasure.

'Aha,' crowed Hal. 'You're smiling at last. So the way to a porcupine's heart is through her cooking.'

'Not necessarily.' She made an unsuccessful attempt to stifle a chuckle. 'I do enjoy having someone to cook for, though.'

'Sounds promising, Jerry,' remarked Hal out of the side of his mouth. 'Do you suppose we can get Belinda to ask us again?'

Jerry grinned. 'Well, she likes bicycle-riding. She told me. And so do you, Dad, so you could take her cycling and then crash into her bike so we'd have to fix it. Then we could bring it back to her and maybe she'd ask us in to eat.'

'I'm not in the habit of crashing into my customers,' said Hal. 'They don't like it. Not that there's any need to sabotage the lady's bike, Jerry. She can do a thorough job of that without my help.'

'That's not fair,' snapped Belinda. 'I've always looked after it myself and I've never had any problems before.'

'All right. Point taken.' Hal laughed and held up his hands to ward off the fork she was waving under his nose. 'I admit your bike's in very good repair—considering.'

'Considering what?' Belinda was still belligerent.

'Its age mostly. I can see it's had a lot of use. You must like exercise.'

'What makes you say that?'

He shrugged. 'Bicycle-riding, walking in the park—or don't you do that any more?' His eyes were suddenly very bright and probing.

Belinda stared at her plate. 'I . . . I . . . guess I haven't lately.'

'I noticed.'

She kept her eyes on the plate.

'Look at me, Belinda.'

Reluctantly, and feeling incredibly foolish, she looked up to meet his demand.

'*Have* you been staying away deliberately? Because you didn't want to meet me?' There was no avoiding the question. The dark intensity of his gaze seemed to bore right into her brain.

'Yes,' she said, in a very small voice. 'I guess I have.'

'Why?' His voice was as quiet as hers. Quiet and hard.

'I don't know.'

Hal saw that her face, which had been attractively flushed most of the evening, had returned to its usual pallor, and her big brown eyes were enormous and filled with a sort of fear. He felt an unexpected sensation in his chest, and knew with a jolt of surprise that he didn't want this funny, grey young woman to be frightened. Especially not frightened of him.

'It's all right,' he said softly. 'You don't have to answer. Not if you don't want to.'

Belinda didn't want to, but it was mainly because she found she was unable to speak.

Hal waited a moment, then went on as if nothing had happened. 'Perhaps I'll see you in the park tomorrow then. I usually have a run before work.'

Again Belinda didn't answer, but this time it was because Jerry had interrupted. 'Yeah, and Grandma says that's another thing. You wear yourself out running in circles because you don't know how to keep still.'

Hal scowled. 'I don't wear myself out. And Grandma's a very bad influence. What other discreditable things does she tell you about your father?'

'That she didn't send you to college so you could lie on the floor fixing bicycles and getting yourself covered in grease. She says you ought to leave all that to your employees.'

'I rarely lie on the floor. And I happen to like fixing bicycles.'

'I know,' Jerry said. 'That's what makes Grandma mad.'

'Everything makes Grandma mad,' said Hal resignedly. 'At the moment I'm not Mrs Blake's favourite son.'

'You're her only son.' Jerry frowned, puzzled. 'Since Grandpa died she says you and me are all she has left.'

'Don't I know it?' He sighed. 'Why can't she play bingo or bridge like other grandmas, and let me get on with my life?'

'She doesn't like bingo or bridge. She likes organising people. Just like you do, Dad.'

Belinda choked into her coffee and Hal gave her a reproving glare.

'So much for filial respect,' he muttered. 'Not to mention respect from one's hostess.'

Belinda began to see that discussing intimate family concerns in front of other people and children was considered entirely normal behaviour in the Blake family.

Shortly afterwards Hal thanked Belinda for the meal and said he must be getting home. Belinda saw them to the door, promised to phone to check on Jerry's ankle and, feeling as if she had been zapped by a tornado, sank down at the kitchen table and covered her face with her hands.

It had been an evening like no other she could remember. Exhausting, exciting, frustrating—and yet companionable somehow. There was something to be said for having someone to cook for—and to talk to and to laugh with. As long as it doesn't become a habit, she reminded herself emphatically. Hal was not a habit she felt she could afford.

The next day she rang Blake's shop and was assured, briefly, that yes, Jerry had a sprained ankle and would not be returning to Victoria as planned. Hal was so abrupt that Belinda decided he must either be exceptionally busy, or in an exceptionally bad temper.

She thanked him with equal abruptness, and this time it was her turn to hang up the phone in his ear.

The following morning she got up, looked out of the window at the bright, sunny morning, and decided that no tiresome hunk called Hal Blake was going to keep her and Misty from enjoying their walk.

She slipped on the grey track-suit, ran a half-hearted comb through her hair, made a quick phone call to Joe who always kept an eye on the animals and, before she could change her mind, had pulled the truck out into the lane and was heading for the park behind the town.

She had already been once round the trail and was just beginning to relax and enjoy the music coming through her earphones when she sensed feet thudding on the turf behind her. A moment later a familiar figure in shorts hurtled past her, stopped, turned around and stood squarely in the middle of the path.

CHAPTER THREE

BELINDA didn't stop at once, but her steps became slower and slower, and finally she was forced to a halt. Hal was making no attempt to move except to take off his earphones, and there was no way she could get around him without pushing her way through the bush.

She found herself staring at the black T-shirt stretched across his chest. Then her eyes dropped lower, past brief black shorts to solid thighs and long, muscular legs. Nice legs, she thought approvingly, not too hairy but just right. All of him was just right really—as no doubt he was all too well aware.

She raised her eyes, saw that his lips were moving and, unwillingly, lifted her hands to push her earphones to the back of her head.

'Good morning, Belinda.' That voice again. Her stomach gave a brief, uneasy flutter.

'Good morning.' Now she was staring at his feet. Big feet, in battered white runners.

'Something interesting down there?' he taunted gently.

'No. I . . .' Belinda looked up quickly and saw that his mouth was curved in a smile. A curling, sensuous smile. The sort of smile that was an obvious invitation.

'How's Jerry?' she demanded, drawing her breath in sharply.

Hal pulled his face straight immediately. 'Coming along very well. I expect he'll be back at school by next week. He's beginning to get bored with his own company for one thing, and he's not at all impressed by the daytime fare on TV.'

'No, I shouldn't think so.' Belinda smiled, relieved that the conversation had taken a mundane turn. 'I remember I was laid up with mumps once and all I could find to watch were talk shows, cooking shows and soaps. I expect Jerry prefers more action.'

'He does. Car chases, shoot-outs, invasions from outer space—anything with the requisite quota of blood and gore.' Hal raised a hand to his jaw and fixed his eyes on her with suspicious gravity. 'I presume your tastes run along the same lines, do they, or you wouldn't have found the talk shows quite so dull.'

'Certainly not.' Belinda tried to look indignant and found herself laughing instead. 'I was hoping for something suitably uplifting. Naturally.' She tilted her nose and looked loftily into the air.

'Good lord. How intimidating.'

'Good,' said Belinda primly. 'And now will you please be intimidated into getting out of my way?'

To her amazement, her words were accompanied by a resounding blare of trumpets, as the third movement of Khachaturyan's Violin Concerto reverberated upwards through the trees. She jumped, and hastily turned off her headset. She had forgotten that her choice of music was no longer her personal concern, although three disgusted crows did not hesitate to voice their opinion of the disturbance.

Hal, who had irritatingly remembered to switch off his set, grinned at her and remarked that there was no need to deafen the wildlife. 'And I'll certainly consider moving without the fanfare of trumpets,' he assured her solemnly.

Which was all very well, but he was still blocking the path so that she couldn't get by.

Belinda sighed. 'Then would you please do it?'

'Do what?'

'Move, of course.'

'In a minute. Do you always listen to that kind of music?'

'Mostly. I prefer it. Don't you?' She gestured at the earphones in his hand.

'No. I prefer Hank Williams, Dwight Yoakum, Willie Nelson . . .'

'Oh,' said Belinda dismissively. 'Country and western. I suppose it's a kind of music.'

'Yes, country and western. And there's no need to take that tone with me, madam.'

'What tone?' she asked defensively.

'The sort of tone that leaves me in no doubt that you think my taste is in my . . .'

'I don't care where your taste is, Mr Blake,' she interrupted hastily. Then, as she saw his eyes watching her with thinly veiled amusement, she added with a slightly sheepish smile, 'You're right, though. I didn't mean to be superior. You are perfectly entitled to listen to whatever you like.'

'How generous of you. It's not to be earphones at dawn, then?'

Belinda laughed. She had been laughing a lot this morning. 'No. No earphones at dawn. Did I really sound as priggish as that?'

'Worse. But I forgive you.'

'How generous of you, Mr Blake.'

'Hal.'

'Hal,' she repeated hesitantly.

He heaved a loud, overdramatic sigh. 'Another hurdle overcome. We *are* coming along this morning, aren't we, Belinda?'

'No,' said Belinda dampeningly. 'As a matter of fact

we're not. We're standing in the middle of the trail and getting nowhere. And maybe you're not in a hurry, but I have animals to feed. Come on, Misty.'

Hal stared at her and his expression was hard to interpret. He always looked intense when he wasn't smiling, but there was something else now, something enigmatic that she didn't understand. Briefly, it came to her that perhaps he didn't understand it either. Then she dismissed the thought as fanciful, because if there was one thing she was sure of, it was that Hal Blake didn't suffer from self-doubt.

The object of her musings shifted to the side of the trail, and Belinda noted that even that small motion accentuated his superb figure, and the cat-like, almost sinuous way he moved.

She swallowed, mumbled, 'Goodbye, then,' and was about to step past him when a disturbing thought brought her up short.

'Jerry,' she said, pausing as she came level with him. 'He isn't by himself all day, is he? Because . . .'

'No,' replied Hal. 'My neighbour, Mrs Oliphant, keeps an eye on him. And I go home to see to his lunch. My new manager is—managing quite well.'

'Oh. That's all right then.' The picture she had of Hal as the restless, self-confident boss of all he surveyed didn't quite fit with this other picture of Hal the concerned father, hurrying home to make lunch for his injured son.

But that odd look was back in his eyes again as he asked now, 'Why? Were you going to offer . . .?'

Belinda started to shake her head, then nodded instead. 'Yes, although I doubt if he'd find my company much of an improvement on television.'

'If he didn't, he'd be a damn young fool,' said Hal

with surprising violence.

Belinda gaped at him, startled. Then, before he could confuse her further, she beckoned to Misty and scurried away along the path.

Hal watched her go, frowning. What was it about this strange young woman that induced thoughts he hadn't had for years? His mother had been right when she accused him of concentrating his attentions on decorative ladies with busts, long legs and swaying hips. He knew where he was with that sort, and they wanted the same thing as he did. Bed without commitment, in return for some wining and dining and the odd expensive present. Since Dolores had left him that had been all the commitment he needed and, whatever his mother said, he had no wish at all to rock a perfectly convenient boat. Well, just occasionally he had dreams . . . No. Only trouble lay in that direction, as he ought to know better than most.

Belinda . . . He shook his head, pulled on his earphones and jogged purposefully down the trail. Belinda was small, always in grey, not beautiful, although when one got to know her her elfin looks did have a certain charm . . . But she wasn't his type. He pushed damp, dark hair back off his forehead. No, definitely not his type.

As Belinda mixed up pet food and released the dogs for their run, she was thinking much the same thing.

Hal had a very obvious charm, but he certainly wasn't her type—because she didn't have a type. There was just no place for the opposite sex on her carefully organised agenda. Well, no place for *young* members of the opposite sex, she amended as she glanced across the kitchen and saw old Joe settling himself comfortably down for a chat.

'You get that bike fixed?' he demanded, as if she were a small girl who rarely obeyed her elders.

'Yes, I did, Joe.'

'Hm. And what did you think of Hal Blake?'

'He knows how to fix bikes.'

'Should hope so. He's made a fortune at it.'

Belinda lifted her head from the unappetising mixture in front of her. 'Is he very rich then? He doesn't look it.'

'Huh. And how do you go about looking rich then, missy?'

'Oh, I don't know. I suppose—I suppose I think of rich men in evening dress and diamond tie-pins or attending board meetings in pin-striped suits to talk about making more money. But Hal wears jeans and denim shirts and—and shorts—and he never talks about money.'

'Hmm-mm.' Joe's bushy eyebrows beetled at her suspiciously, and she realised she had said altogether too much. Joe's matchmaking efforts on her behalf had never got anywhere before, so he was bound to think that the fact she knew Hal wore shorts was progress. Better change the subject. Now.

But instead she found herself asking curiously, 'Since you know so much about everything that goes on here, Joe, does Hal rent that house next to the Oliphants? I thought it was up for sale.'

'It was. He bought it, so I'm told.'

'Oh. That's odd, you know, because Jerry says . . .'

'Jerry?' The eyebrows beetled so busily that she couldn't see his eyes.

'His son.'

'Whose son?'

'Hal's son.' This conversation was becoming ludicrous.

'Huh. What does Jerry say?'

'He says Hal never stays anywhere for long.'

'Dare say. But a man like that wouldn't want to be bothered with renting. Landlords coming round to complain about holes in the wall—all that sort of nonsense.'

'Holes in the wall?' said Belinda in astonishment. 'Oh, I see what you mean. For pictures and things like that.' No, she couldn't see Hal taking kindly to complaining landlords either. If he wanted to punch holes in the wall, for pictures or anything else, then that was exactly what he would do.

'You going to see him again?' asked the old man. Joe had never let the fact that something was none of his business interfere with a natural tendency to meddle.

'No,' said Belinda quickly, turning her head away so that he couldn't see her face. 'Why should I?'

Behind her she heard fingers tap impatiently on the table. 'Because you need friends, Bella. Young friends.'

'I don't need friends, Joe. I've got you, and I've got Misty and the animals. Are you staying for breakfast?' Maybe food would get his mind off her concerns.

'Nope.' Suddenly he was in a thoroughly bad temper. 'Got things to do. You're a fool, Bella.' Clearing his throat noisily he got up from the table and clumped off through the door and down the steps.

Belinda looked after him and smiled resignedly. She loved Joe, didn't know what she would do without him, but sometimes his bullying and grumbling did get a little hard to take. Perhaps it was just as well he wasn't staying for breakfast.

She knew why he was angry, though. It was because he couldn't get his way about her and Hal.

She laughed without much mirth. Belinda Ballantyne and Hal Blake. What a ridiculous notion. Old Joe really must be going round the bend.

Funny though. Just for a moment the idea hadn't seemed particularly ridiculous. Fantastic maybe, but not ridiculous. And it had filled her with a pleasant little glow. Then the glow had faded as reality had taken over.

Belinda lifted the pan of dog food, walked out to the kennels and slammed it to the ground in front of three startled but happily hungry dogs.

'Your musical tastes appear to be on the classically noisy side,' remarked a low voice from the window. 'By the way, I do approve of the view. Very tempting.'

It was the following evening, just around supper time, and Belinda, wearing blue jeans beneath her inevitable grey sweatshirt and watched anxiously by Misty, was kneeling on her blue-patterned rug with an arm stretched as far as it would reach beneath the sofa. Her head was twisted sideways as she tried to grasp the object of her search.

Hal, who was standing on the grass outside the open window, smiled appreciatively as her neat little bottom wriggled backwards. She sat up looking flushed, and with her normally tidy hair in disarray.

'What are you doing here?' she asked rudely, in no mood to make polite social noises after being discovered in this undignified position. 'I didn't hear you drive up.'

'I'm not surprised.' He waved a hand at her stereo system which was emitting the rousing military finale to Tchaikovsky's 1812 Overture. 'And what I was doing was admiring a particularly delectable view. You should wear those jeans more often.'

Belinda's flush deepened. Unlike most young women her age, she had had almost no experience at coping with this kind of innuendo, and it made her acutely uncomfortable.'

Hal, noting her discomfort, went on more seriously, 'You have a nice figure under those appallingly baggy sweatshirts, Belinda. Why don't you show it more often?'

Belinda leaned back against the sofa and pulled awkwardly at her sweatshirt. 'I—I don't . . .' She ran her tongue over lips that had gone suddenly dry. 'Mr—Hal . . . I don't think my clothes are any of your business.'

'Maybe not.' He rested his hip on the window ledge and crossed his arms on his chest. 'On the other hand, if they were, I should positively forbid you to wear so much as a shadow of grey. It doesn't suit you.'

'You don't have the right to forbid me, Hal Blake. And I happen to be fond of grey.'

'Too bad. It makes you look like an undernourished mouse.'

It was said with a smile, but she knew he meant it. And his words brought a recollection of Jerry's cheerfully unguarded comment that his father had said he had plans to pounce on the mouse. Quite suddenly she didn't feel mouselike at all. She was tired of Hal's arrogant assumption that he had a right to tell her what to wear. And she was tired of being told she wasn't attractive. As if she didn't know it!

'I'm not interested in your opinion, thank you,' she said sharply. 'In fact, I'm not particularly interested in you.' She became conscious that the record was still going round in circles, and she got up to turn it off. When she turned around Hal was no longer at the window.

Her hand went to her mouth and her eyes widened. He couldn't have disappeared as fast as that.

He hadn't. A moment later she heard the unlocked kitchen door slam shut, and then Hal was standing in front of her with his arms held loosely at his sides. He looked very male and overpowering staring down at her in the small, feminine room. Like some dark, magnetic and probably ill-intentioned spirit who didn't belong in the quiet, rustic atmosphere of her home. He had brought something very physical in with him, an electricity, a sensuality that was quite new to her and, in a surprising way, exhilarating.

Belinda breathed in deeply and stood still.

Slowly Hal lifted his hands and placed them on her shoulders. A shock ran through her body and she flinched.

'Why are you afraid of me, Belinda?'

'I—I'm not afraid of you.'

'Yes, you are. You're quivering like a little cornered mouse.'

Oh, yes. The mouse again. The one he was going to pounce on. Not if she had anything to do with it, he wasn't. And she was not really afraid of him—only of what he was capable of doing to her carefully constructed defences. But she *was* afraid of the new and unexpected feelings he aroused in her, even just by being in the same room.

His hands were still touching her, his thumbs revolving slowly around her shoulderblades.

'I'm not a mouse,' she said quickly. 'I may look like one, Hal, but looks can be deceptive. So you can forget any ideas you had about playing the big, bad cat.'

Hal's hands dropped abruptly, and she was irritated to find she missed them. 'Of course,' he said curtly. 'I forgot about my son and his big mouth.'

'If you kept your own mouth shut in front of him, you

wouldn't have to worry about it, would you?' said Belinda.

For a moment he just glared at her, saying nothing. Then the angry lines which twisted his mouth faded, and after a while he gave her a rueful smile.

'You're a hundred per cent right about that, Belinda. But you see, sometimes I forget. I've been alone a lot since my—since Dolores left me. I don't always remember that Jerry is only a child. Besides . . .' He sighed. 'What I don't say to him, my mother will.'

So Hal's wife had left him, thought Belinda. That would have been a blow to his ego—maybe even to his heart? 'It must be difficult for you,' she agreed, her voice softening.

Hal, watching her face, saw the pansy eyes darken with sympathy, and suddenly he thought, my goodness, I was wrong. She *is* beautiful. Then he remembered that, thanks to Jerry's revelations and his own thoughtlessness, she probably had him pegged as some kind of lecherous ogre bent on seduction. Not a totally unfair conclusion either, he admitted wryly. He *had* considered finding out how far he could go with her. Not that his intentions had ever really progressed as far as seduction. Until very recently he had been much too convinced that Belinda was not his type.

'It is difficult sometimes,' he answered her. 'But that's no excuse for what I said to Jerry.'

'It's all right,' said Belinda. 'It doesn't matter.'

'It does if you're still afraid of me. It was just a foolish and remarkably arrogant comment, made at the end of a long and busy day. I apologise.'

'Apology accepted. And I'm not afraid of you. Why should I be?'

'No reason at all. And I promise I won't attack you

without your consent.'

Belinda smiled. 'You won't get it, you know,' she told him.

'That's too bad. And that view I had through the window looked so promising.'

Belinda glanced up quickly and saw that although he was grinning at her, there was a strange look of confusion in his eyes. But then he was a strange man, wasn't he? Not nearly as easy to fathom as she had imagined when she first met him. Then she had taken him for a confident, self-satisfied stud and nothing more. The kind of man who saw himself as God's gift to women.

'Won't you sit down?' she asked now, gesturing vaguely behind her, and taking refuge in formality.

Hal glanced doubtfully at the blue and white, chintz-covered sofa. 'Depends.'

'What do you mean?'

'I'm not sitting on anything in this house until I know what might be underneath it.'

'Oh.' Belinda laughed. 'It's all right. No rats, snakes or gerbils. I was only trying to get at Misty's ball.'

'So that was it. Here, hang on a minute.'

Suddenly Hal was stretched out on the rug, his long arms extended beneath the sofa. Belinda stared down at him, at the rebellious hair curling at the base of his neck, then over the impressive denim shoulders to his waist. Then further . . . mm. Very appealing.

She was just beginning to berate herself for harbouring thoughts she had neither wanted nor expected, when Hal levered himself up on his arms and rose easily to his feet.

'There. One ball. Slightly hairy, but no doubt Misty will think it's all the better for that. Won't you, Misty?'

He bent down to scratch the lopsided dog behind her ear, and Misty gazed up at him with traitorous adoration.

'Thank you.' Belinda took the ball and put it by the door in Misty's basket, where its owner promptly retreated to guard it. She wished that for once she had thought to vacuum the inevitable clumps of fur beneath the furniture.

But Hal didn't seem to care. 'Now I'll sit down,' he said, sinking on to the sofa, and looking alluringly ruffled after the treasure hunt on the floor. He patted the cushion beside him. 'Come and join me.'

Belinda hesitated, but knowing that if she refused it would only confirm his suspicions that she was a mouse, in the end she sat as far away from him as possible, with the arms of the sofa pressed uncomfortably into her back.

'Would you like some coffee?' she asked hopefully.

'No, thank you.'

There went that avenue of escape.

'What—what *do* you want, then?' He had promised that pouncing was out, so the question seemed relatively safe.

Unfortunately at that moment her eyes strayed unwittingly to the firm male thigh relaxing so close to her own, and immediately she could think of nothing but his nearness and the faint, clean scent of his soap. When she began to take in the fact that he was saying something, she was certain she must have heard wrong, so she asked him to say it again.

'I said do you have a dress that isn't grey?'

So she hadn't heard wrong after all.

'Why?' she asked blankly.

His full lips parted so that she could just see the white teeth gleaming against his skin, and his voice was very deep and persuasive.

'Because I have to attend a charity ball in Vancouver next weekend, and I'd like you to come with me, Belinda—that is, if you promise me faithfully that you won't show up dressed in grey.'

CHAPTER FOUR

BELINDA stared at him, not really believing. The last time she had been taken to a dance by a man—no, boy really—it had been an unmitigated disaster, and she had never felt the smallest inclination to try her luck again. So how was it that this disconcerting, fascinating, rich and successful bicycle baron suddenly wanted *her* as his partner at a glitzy charity ball? It could hardly be because of her charm and sophistication—and, as he had made abundantly clear, it wasn't because he admired her style, or the way she wore her clothes . . . Her clothes.

Something stirred in Belinda then, as she took in his expectant face and recalled his cool assumption that he had a right to tell her what to wear. Something that was a return of her old independence and the unassuming confidence which had enabled her to solve most of the problems which life had thrown her way. All right, so she was quiet and inclined to be solitary, she conceded, but she wasn't particularly shy and she certainly wasn't some vapid clinging vine he could push around at will—just because he had condescended to invite her to some fancy affair in Vancouver.

To which she wasn't going.

'Thank you for asking,' she replied with careful composure. 'It's very kind of you. But you needn't worry about being seen with a woman who doesn't fit your dress code, Hal, because of course I can't possibly accept.'

'Why not?' His fingers tapped impatiently against his

thigh and she could tell from the abruptness of the question that he wasn't used to being turned down.

'Because I don't have anything to wear,' she replied with deliberate sarcasm. Then, watching him, she felt a quiver of satisfaction at the surprised chagrin that was evident in the sudden sparking of his eyes.

Oh, it would do him good not to get his own way for a change. She smiled complacently.

'I see,' he said now. 'I've offended you, haven't I? I'm sorry. I didn't intend to.' His words were clipped, and she realised that apologies did not come easily to him.

'You haven't offended me, Hal,' she said quietly. 'It's just that balls really aren't my style. And anyway I don't go out with men.'

When she saw the look of dawning suspicion in his eyes, she added hastily, 'I don't go out with anyone—except Joe sometimes or one or two girls from school—and my dog.'

'Joe?' His voice was flat, uninterested.

'Joe's my neighbour. He's an artist—and he's almost seventy-five,' she finished drily, as she saw his lean body stiffen in a way that was irritatingly seductive.

'Almost seventy-five?' The large frame relaxed visibly, and the beginnings of a smile began to play about his mouth.

Heavens, thought Belinda. It's almost as if he actually cares who I go out with. But of course that's completely ridiculous. Out of the question. It's just that there aren't many unattached women in Cinnamon Bay, and it's easier for him to ask me to the ball than to spend time on the telephone tracking down one of his leggy ladies in Victoria or Vancouver.

Surprisingly, he grinned at her, and stretched out long, muscular legs as he rested his head comfortably on the back of the sofa. His dark hair seemed almost alive against the pristine blue and white.

'If I've offended you, Belinda, I do apologise. I had no business telling you what to wear.' When she didn't answer he added with a slight grimace, 'All the same, you really do look terrible in grey. Please come with me.' Smiling, he reached over to take her hand.

The famous Blake charm in action, she thought sourly, snatching it quickly away.

'I can't. I couldn't leave my animals. And anyway I really don't have anything to wear. Not even anything grey.'

'Thank heaven for that. And of course you can leave your animals. Your friend Joe would take care of them, wouldn't he? Or someone from the town?'

She shook her head. 'No.'

'Why not?'

'Because—because I don't want to ask them. Thank you.'

Hal let his breath out on a long, exasperated sigh. 'All right. If that's the way you feel; Belinda, I'm sorry to have taken up your time.' Before she could think of a way to soften her refusal, he had uncoiled his body and risen lithely to his feet.

Belinda, knowing that she could have handled this situation more graciously, stood up too so that he wouldn't seem quite so large and disconcerting.

'Thank you for asking,' she repeated in a small voice.

He shrugged. 'No problem. Goodnight.'

'Would—would you like to stay for supper?' She had to say something to make amends for what he obviously regarded as an ill-mannered rejection of his generous invitation.

Hal shook his head. 'No, thank you. I have to get back

to Jerry. See you around.'

Before she could do more than open her mouth he had spun away from her and was striding out through the door. It slammed, and a few seconds later she heard his truck start. Then it was tearing down the lane in a shower of flying gravel.

Idiot, she thought, as she wandered into the kitchen. If he keeps on driving like that, I hope it's only his own stiff neck he breaks.

It wasn't true though. As she reached listlessly for a saucepan to start supper, she knew with a shock of horrifying clarity that she would be quite devastated if anything happened to Hal.

In the end, the prospect of his mangled body lying crumpled at the side of the road turned out to be quite enough to ruin her meal—which by the time she got round to eating it was only rather cold, semi-congealed scrambled egg.

It was still early when she finished clearing away the dishes, but now her listlessness had turned into a restless inability to keep still. She drifted into the small bathroom and, feeling slightly self-conscious, stared into the mirror to make a careful inspection of her face. No. It hadn't changed. It was the same old pale face with the wide mouth, pointed chin—even pointed ears. And her hair was the same old curly black mop that took so little trouble to control. Obviously, as she had known all along, it wasn't her fabulous looks that had prompted Hal's startling invitation.

Dispiritedly she turned away and called to Misty. Then she phoned Joe again and, with the little dog trotting behind, took off slowly down the lane on her bike. She could see the marks of Hal's tyres in the gravel.

At first she had no idea where she was going, but in

the end she found herself pedalling dreamily through the town, and when nothing there held her interest she continued on to the beach.

The sun had almost disappeared, and only wisps of orange trailed across the skyline to touch the hazy shapes of the offshore islands with a soft, amber glow. The sea breeze rippled through her hair and lifted it on her neck as Misty raced across the sand in pursuit of a seagull which turned out to be only a disappointing piece of driftwood.

Belinda drew in a long, salt-tanged breath. This was better. Out here, in the peace and semi-darkness, her head seemed clearer. Perhaps now she might be able to think like the sane and intelligent woman she knew she was.

Why had she refused Hal's invitation? Was he right, and was she afraid of him? No, she decided, as a small sailing boat bobbed darkly on the water in the distance. No, it wasn't that. On the whole she trusted him—and in any case she certainly trusted herself. But she *didn't* want her life to be disrupted. She liked it the way it was. And she was becoming increasingly aware that Hal had the power to disrupt her in all kinds of unexpected ways. Her refusal *had* been based partly on the fact that glitzy Vancouver balls were not her style. But that wasn't the whole story. Her main reason for turning him down had been the knowledge that any continuation of her acquaintance with the owner of Blake's Bicycles was likely to involve her in exactly the kind of emotional shot-blast that had hit her when she had just turned eighteen.

Belinda watched the sun vanish completely into the black bulk of the islands. Of course she was older now. Older and wiser. And anyway her heart hadn't been seriously involved all those years ago. Only her vulnerable, adolescent feelings.

She sighed. Remembering that other experience didn't help much, because she knew instinctively that with Hal it might not be so easy to keep her heart intact. And as her father had always told her, love, and particularly marriage, were traps to be avoided at all costs.

She believed him.

Whistling to Misty, Belinda jumped back on to her bike. Yes, she had made the right decision. Of course she had. No question.

Why was it though, she wondered, as she pedalled up the hill from the beach, why was it that this eminently sensible conclusion seemed to give her no comfort whatever?

She was still wondering when the phone rang insistently just as she was heading out of the door the next morning.

Leaving Misty sitting forlornly in the doorway, she hurried irritably across the kitchen to pick it up. Who on earth could be calling her at this uncivilised hour? It was barely six o'clock.

'Belinda? It's Hal.'

Of course. She might have known. But she hadn't. She had expected him to give up on her after last night.

'Yes?' she said cautiously.

'I won't be seeing you in the park this morning. I have to go into the shop early because my new manager is having a tooth pulled.'

'Oh. Poor man.' Did he really think she cared whether she saw him in the park or not? She hadn't even considered the possibility, had she? Yes, murmured a tiresome little voice in her head. She had.

'Mm, it's unfortunate. Never mind, he expects to be

back tomorrow. That's why I'm calling.'

'Oh?' This conversation wasn't making much sense.

'Yes. He knows quite enough to handle the shop for an afternoon, so I thought we might go for a picnic.' When she didn't answer, he added impatiently, 'You're not going to tell me that picnics are not your style?'

'No—no. But—it's April.'

'I know what month it is, Belinda.'

'Yes, but people don't go on picnics in April.'

'I do. And it's an exceptionally warm April.'

'I suppose so, but—my animals.'

'For Pete's sake, Belinda, your friend can look after them for a couple of hours. Mrs Barclay tells me he does it frequently, and that when he can't make it Jack Oliphant fills in for you.'

'Thank *you*, Mrs Barclay,' said Belinda viciously.

There was silence on the other end of the line, and for a moment Belinda thought he had hung up. Contrarily, she hoped he hadn't. Then his voice whipped back across the wires. 'And thank *you*, Miss Ballantyne. For making it crystal-clear that my company doesn't appeal to you.'

'No,' cried Belinda, her voice cracking with distress. 'No, Hal, it's not that at all. At least . . .'

'At least *what*?'

'I—I don't know. I do like your company. It's just that . . .'

She heard him draw in his breath, before he said in a curiously flat, indifferent voice, 'I'm sure Jerry would like you to come, Belinda.'

'Oh. Oh, *Jerry's* going?'

'Does that make a difference?' The flat, clipped note was more noticeable than ever.

'No. I mean—well, yes, if Jerry wants me to go . . .'

'All right then. I'll pick you up at two o'clock.' Now

he sounded as if the whole thing was a bore.

'Yes. Thank you,' she agreed doubtfully.

Hal hung up the phone with a snap.

From the doorway Misty gave a hopeful whimper. 'Yes, I'm coming,' Belinda assured her. 'You're not going to miss your run because I had a phone call.'

An unexpected phone call, she mused, as she wandered down the lane. She had been sure that after her refusal to go to the ball with Hal he wouldn't bother to waste time on her again. But perhaps the picnic had been Jerry's idea. And of course she couldn't disappoint Jerry.

At least that was what she told herself as she stared glumly into her wardrobe the next morning. The important thing was not to upset Jerry, who must be sorely in need of an outing after his enforced and unhappy acquaintance with daytime fare on TV.

She did not pause to consider, as she riffled frantically through her clothes in search of colour, that it was not Jerry who had said she looked terrible in grey, but his father.

And *her* father had told her that shades of grey suited her. No, she amended, not suited her exactly. What he had actually said was that if she didn't dress to attract, she would save herself a lot of grief and heartache. He had warned her that any kind of relationship with a man would change her contented, happy life for the worse. At the time she hadn't cared to mention that life with him was not noticeably happy or contented. As he grew older and more bitter, he had also become more short-tempered and opinionated by the day, and she had learned quickly that there was nothing to be gained by disagreeing with him.

It wasn't until after he died that it occurred to her he

was probably more interested in retaining her unpaid housekeeping services than he was in her happiness and well-being. But by that time her habit of wearing unobtrusive clothing had become second nature, and she had decided for her own reasons that love and marriage would never be for her.

Her hands groped at the back of the old mahogany wardrobe and finally fell on something that wasn't grey. She eyed it doubtfully. Would Hal like this very practical garment any better? Belinda frowned. Well, if he didn't, it was just too bad. She buttoned up the sensible shirt, tucked it into the jeans he had condescended to approve, and plugged in the kettle to make her ninth cup of coffee for the day.

'All that caffeine's bad for you,' muttered Joe an hour later, as he cast a disgruntled eye over the array of cups in Belinda's dishpan. 'You should take better care of yourself, Bella.'

'I don't usually drink this much coffee,' she excused herself. 'But if you want the truth, Joe, I'm nervous.'

'Huh. Nothing to be nervous about. Hal Blake's a nice young man.'

'I know. It's not that . . .'

It wasn't either. She was not afraid of Hal. But, as she was just beginning to realise, she was almost afraid of herself.

Although in one way she was dreading Hal's arrival, it was almost a relief when his truck pulled up in front a few seconds later, preventing Joe from making any further comments about her coffee consumption.

As usual, Hal was wearing jeans, but the denim shirt had been discarded in favour of a dark blue woollen sweater which clung softly to his body and provided a tempting glimpse of the dark, muscled sinews at his neck.

Belinda dug her nails into her palms. 'Where's Jerry?'

Hal raised his eyes to study the tops of the trees. 'Mrs Oliphant was going down to Victoria this morning, and, as Jerry's ankle is so much better, I sent him along with her to join his grandmother.'

'I see.' Belinda stared at him, and found that his attention was still riveted on the trees. 'You said he was coming with us,' she accused him.

'I know I did. I lied.' He lowered his eyes and gave her what she supposed was meant to be a disarming grin.

Behind her Belinda heard a sound that was a cross between a cough and a chuckle. She scowled. Old Joe would get his later! Right now she had Hal to deal with.

But in the end it was Hal who dealt with her.

'I'm not going, then,' she told him flatly.

'Yes, you are . . .'

'Don't be a fool, girl . . .'

Hal and Joe both spoke at once.

'I'm not going. And I'm not a fool.'

'You are, and you are a fool.' There was a purposeful glint in Hal's eyes now, and the muscles in his face were pulled tight as he stepped towards her. Before she had any idea what he intended, he had swept her up in his arms and dumped her unceremoniously on the passenger seat of the truck. Then he slammed the door, locked it and leaped into the seat beside her.

Immediately Belinda reached for the handle, rattled it, and found it wouldn't move.

'Don't waste your time. I had kiddie locks installed years ago when Jerry first learned to cause trouble. This truck is older than it looks.' Hal's smile was a study in maddening complacency as he started up the engine and reversed out into the lane.

Through the open window on his side, she heard Joe shout after them, 'Bravo, son. Well done. That's the way to handle her.'

'Bastard,' swore Belinda, glaring at the smugly curling lips on the side of Hal's face that she could see.

'Who? Me or your friend Joe?'

'Both of you. Mainly you.'

'Good. Always glad to give satisfaction.'

'You are *not* giving satisfaction. And I can assure you that mauling me about like a sack of used bicycle parts is not the way to handle me, whatever Joe may think.'

'No, I don't suppose it is. And I can assure *you* that the caveman style is not an approach I particularly favour myself. Besides, it just wouldn't look right if I tried dragging you around by the hair. It's much too short, for one thing.'

'Oh! Of all the . . . '

'Mm, and by the way, I don't actually have sacks of used bicycle parts,' he interrupted blandly.

'Hal Blake, you turn this truck around this minute. I insist on being taken home right now.'

'Insist all you like. You're not going anywhere. I didn't go to all this trouble for nothing.'

'Nobody asked you to go to any trouble. You're an arrogant, rude, unprincipled, conceited . . .'

'I know. Bastard,' Hal finished for her smugly.

'*Precisely*. And so's Joe.'

'Don't be too hard on Joe.' He turned his face towards her, and she saw a warmth in it that hadn't been there before. 'I'm sure he only has your welfare at heart.'

'Huh. And I suppose you have too.'

'Believe it or not, I have.'

'Oh, sure. That's why you kidnapped me, I suppose.'

He shrugged. 'Desperate situations call for desperate measures.'

'It was hardly a desperate situation, Hal,' scoffed Belinda.

'Wasn't it? How do you know I wasn't desperate?'

Something in his voice made her look at him closely, but all she could see was the hard line of his profile staring straight ahead at the road.

She didn't bother to reply, and for the remainder of the drive only a vibrant silence quivered in the air between them. It was not broken until they pulled into the car park at Englishman River Falls.

There Hal jumped out of his seat, strode round to her side of the truck and made a slow and deliberate production of unlocking her door.

By the time it was finally open and he had reached out a hand to help her down, Belinda was ready to scratch his eyes out. But she didn't get the chance because he was already swinging her to the ground.

When her feet touched gravel, his big hands lingered on her waist and he stared down at her with an expression that was an odd mixture of amusement and surprise and—surely it wasn't desire she saw in his eyes?

'How could I ever have believed you didn't have a waistline?' he mused softly, his fingers gently massaging the fabric of her shirt.

'I don't know, but my waistline is none of your business, so . . .'

He grinned at her, noting the flushed cheeks and indignantly upturned nose. 'Are you about to stamp your feet and say "kindly unhand me, sir"?' he asked interestedly. 'I've never been asked to unhand a lady before.'

'There's always a first time,' said Belinda through

barely parted teeth. 'Maybe the experience will do you good.'

'Very likely.'

'Hal, let me *go*.'

Abruptly Hal did as she asked, and for the second time in her life Belinda was conscious of missing the provocative pleasure of his touch. Then, as she glared up at him, preparing to give him an uncensored opinion of his behaviour, a slight breeze whispered across the open space, and she shivered.

Instantly Hal's dark eyes stopped gleaming with irritating amusement. 'You're cold,' he exclaimed, his words almost an accusation.

'That's stating the obvious,' muttered Belinda. 'What do you expect when you drag me out here without even giving me time to grab a jacket?'

'You're right. Here, take this.' He reached into the back of the truck and pulled out a large, crumpled denim jacket.

Belinda took it silently, resisting the urge to throw it in his face because she really was beginning to feel the cold. It might be an exceptionally warm spring, but all she had on was a thin and not exceptionally warm cotton shirt.

She was pulling the jacket over her shoulders when Hal took it and held it for her. She turned so that she could put her arms in the sleeves, and he eased it on and then stood for a moment with his body against her back and his hands just touching her neck. Then he turned her very gently around and began to fasten the buttons. He had only done half of them when he stopped.

'Oh, lord.' He started to laugh. 'I guess I've only myself to blame if you look on the baggy side now, Belinda.'

It was true. The sleeves hung down below her finger-tips and the bottom of the jacket came almost to her knees. Like some pathetic orphan of the trash cans, thought Hal, surprised at the feeling of tenderness that assaulted him. Belinda might be a twenty-six-year-old orphan, but up until now he had certainly never thought of her as pathetic. Women who thought boa constrictors were charming pets were not pathetic. And because, for the first time in a long time, he was confused by his own feelings, he said roughly, 'Baggy or not, Belinda, I'm afraid it will have to do.' He eyed the collar of her shirt which poked up at a rakish angle beside her ear, and added irrelevantly, 'That shirt you're wearing isn't grey.'

'I'm aware of that,' she replied coldly.

'No,' said Hal, responding to the ice in her tone. 'It's beige. And beige doesn't suit you one damn bit better than grey.'

'Thank you so much for your frank opinion, Hal. Are you by any chance thinking of taking a position as a fashion consultant?' she asked sweetly. She put her head on one side and pretended to give the matter serious consideration. 'On the whole I think you're probably better suited to fixing bicycles. More to do, you know, and you can always leave customer relations to other people.'

'Porcupine power strikes again,' murmured Hal, brushing a finger across her cheek.

To Belinda's fury, he seemed to be laughing at her. She turned away from him so that he couldn't see the hurt in her eyes.

Then, to her amazement, she felt his hand on her shoulder, and found he was spinning her back to face him.

'Come on, Belinda. I'm sorry. I know you're angry with me, but I didn't see any other way . . .'

'To handle me, I suppose,' she interrupted indignantly. 'I'm not actually a dog, you know, Hal.'

'I know you're not. And I've said I'm sorry. But I didn't see any other way to make you come. And somewhere between that day you ran away from me in the park and today, I discovered I very much wanted to know you better, you see.'

'Oh.' Belinda glared at the blue sweater and wished it didn't suit him so well. 'You could have asked me, couldn't you?'

'I did. And you said you weren't coming.'

'That was because you told me Jerry would be with us. And he wasn't. Why did you lie to me, Hal?'

'What else could I do?' He held out his hands, palms upwards. 'You wouldn't have agreed if I hadn't brought Jerry into the picture. Would you?' His eyes held her so that she was unable to look away, and in the end all she could do was admit the truth.

'No . . . I wouldn't'

'You see?' He smiled, a curving, rueful smile that touched her heart.

'Yes, I suppose so. But—why me, Hal? I don't understand.'

'If I promise to tell you, will you stop fighting me, porcupine, and help me spread this load on one of the picnic tables?' He waved at a promising-looking cooler on the floor at the rear of the truck.

All at once Belinda realised she was very hungry. All she had eaten today was a piece of toast—washed down with a great deal too much coffee. 'All right,' she agreed. 'We'll call a truce until after lunch—if you can call it lunch at three in the afternoon.'

'Spoken like a true gourmet,' Hal mocked her. He had seen the hungry look in her eyes and found it surprisingly endearing.

Five minutes later, each holding a handle of the cooler, they were trundling side by side across the car park like Jack and Jill. When they found a suitable polished wooden table by the river they started to unpack the food.

A sense of dreamy unreality gradually took the place of Belinda's earlier indignation. The sun was washing over them through the trees, the breeze was balmy and the river just below them surged like a sheet of flowing silver towards the falls. In the distance they could hear the thunder of water pounding over a precipice, and as they finished unpacking and Hal eased himself on to the bench beside her, Belinda felt as if she were wrapped in a warm and safe cocoon.

She was glad Hal had kidnapped her after all.

'Sausage rolls,' she gloated, as she began opening containers. 'And ham sandwiches, and eggs and butter tarts and—oh, Hal. *Strawberries!* How did you know I have a passion for strawberries?'

'I didn't. But I happen to have a passion for them myself. So you see we do have something in common—besides a taste for earphones and early mornings.'

'Mm,' said Belinda—incoherently because her mouth was full of sandwich, 'I guess we do.'

For a while they ate in a companionable silence, but when Hal produced two glasses and a bottle of Clos de Vougeot, Belinda announced between mouthfuls, 'We have that in common, too.'

'What?'

'Burgundy. My favourite.'

'Oh,' said Hal. He heaved a melodramatic sigh. 'That's a blow. I was hoping to ply you with wine—about which I was sure you knew nothing—wait for it to do its work and then break down your defences when the inevitable weak moment arrived.' The look he gave her now was pure seduction, in spite of an innocently assumed grin.

'Whose weak moment?' asked Belinda with equal innocence.

'Yours, of course.'

She shook her head. 'You're out of luck, then. I rarely have them.' Except where you're concerned, she added silently to herself. 'And for your information, Hal, Joe and I quite often have wine with our meals. My father did too before he died. Rather more than was good for him, I'm afraid.'

'Hmm. As I said, it's a blow.' Hal adopted an expression which reminded Belinda so much of Misty's disgusted face when she saw her mistress take the last bite of a cookie without sharing it that she burst out laughing.

Watching her wide mouth curve up in unaffected delight, and the bright lights sparkling in her beautiful pansy eyes, Hal felt something expand in his chest that he hadn't felt there for years.

Slowly his lips parted in a smile, and he reached out a hand to touch her hair.

'You have lovely hair, Belinda,' he said softly. 'All glossy curls blowing in the wind.' His fingers moved down to trace tantalisingly over her cheeks and around her jawline. She stopped laughing. 'And your skin is so soft—soft and creamy like ivory . . .'

'Which doesn't go with beige or grey,' remarked Belinda drily. 'Is this Plan Two of the operation, Hal?

Seduction with words instead of wine?' She reached for another butter tart and took a large and unromantic bite.

Hal stared at her, his hand falling back on the table. His eyes darkened slightly. Then he said with a tight but still utterly seductive smile, 'I don't think so. On the other hand, if it works . . .' He shrugged.

'It's not going to.'

'I was afraid it wasn't.' He swallowed a strawberry and poured her the last glass of wine.

'And neither is that.' She gave him a guarded smile. When he only shrugged again and said nothing, she said curiously, 'Hal, I know I asked you before—but why me? There must be other women in Cinnamon Bay who would jump at the chance to go out with you.' She pulled absently at a sliver sticking out from the edge of the table. 'Or is it just that I'm more of a challenge?'

'How do you know I like challenges?'

'Because you do. Don't you?'

He shifted restlessly on the bench and placed both hands squarely on the table. 'I suppose you could say so.'

'And was that why you were so determined to make me come?'

Hal lifted his head then to stare up through the trees at the sky. 'I don't know. Perhaps that was part of it . . .' His voice trailed into silence, and then suddenly he was no longer looking at the sky and Belinda found herself mesmerised by the intense, magnetic scrutiny of his eyes.

'Belinda—why should you think I must have some deep, dark reason for wanting to be with you? Don't you know you're—almost beautiful?' He lifted a curl that had blown across her forehead, and the look he gave her now made her heart beat hard against her ribs. 'What's more,' he was going on unbelievably, 'you can be a joy to be with.' He grinned. 'On those rare occasions when you're not firing quills in my direction.'

'Almost beautiful? A joy to . . .' Belinda gulped, and her mouth fell open in a way that she was sure reflected a greater degree of inanity than beauty.

'Yes, love, a joy.' The endearment came out quite naturally. 'You're funny and clever and capable and kind and—I'm beginning to get used to your face.' He smiled encouragingly, because Belinda still looked as if an avalanche had struck her, and then frozen her mouth open in the snow.

'Don't look to amazed.' He was laughing at her, but it was a gentle sort of laughter, not in the least malicious. When he saw that for the moment Belinda seemed bereft of the power of speech, he continued with a note of authority, 'All right, while you're getting over the shock, and if you've *quite* finished eating . . .' now there *was* a faint note of malice in his tone '. . .you can help me to clear up this mess.' He waved his hand at the collection of plastic cartons, wax paper and eggshells which littered the table, and Belinda, returning to earth, realised that his momentary gentleness did not mean that he had lost the habit of command. Apparently he expected her to jump to it, and, because she was still in a state of dazed disbelief, she did. In no time the unsightly debris of their picnic was tidily back in the cooler.

'There's nobody here except us,' remarked Belinda as they stowed the remains in the truck. It was all she could think of to say, and the teasing, perceptive look in Hal's eyes made her feel she had to say something.

'Not surprising. It's the middle of the week and too early for the tourist influx.' He was taking his cue from her and letting the conversation flow into less personal channels. 'Would you like to take a look at the falls?'

'Of course. Isn't that why we came?'

'It's not why I came,' replied Hal enigmatically, and Belinda decided she wasn't pushing *that* subject any further.

It seemed entirely natural that Hal should take her hand. It also seemed natural, she discovered resignedly, that she should feel as if she were being towed along by a gale-force wind as he led her in the direction of the falls. He had been running the first time she saw him, she remembered. Apparently he hardly ever stopped. Jerry had said something of that sort once, hadn't he? Or his grandmother had. Belinda smiled to herself. Raising Hal to manhood must have been a challenge. No wonder Mrs Blake was inclined to be acerbic now that she was getting older and felt she had a right to expect that her restless son would settle down.

By this point in her musings, they had reached the banks of the river, where it flowed in foaming whiteness over the steep drop to a rocky ravine far below. Here, where tree-lined cliffs imprisoned the torrent, a sturdy wooden bridge spanned the waters, and Hal and Belinda paused in the middle to watch nature's grandeur in all its magnificent force. They didn't stay long, though, because a fine, cold spray was misting over the bridge, and Belinda shivered. Immediately Hal put his arm around her and they moved off on to a path which followed the banks of the river to a quiet rock pool below the falls.

Hal sank on to a smooth sloping rock. Then he held out his hands and pulled Belinda down beside him.

For a while they sat quietly side by side staring into the pool—and a great sense of peace came over Belinda. This was strange, because the falls were still thundering round the corner, and Hal was not a peaceful man.

After a long time he turned to her and said with that twisted smile which always set her pulses racing,'I'm glad you came with me today, Belinda. I wouldn't have asked you again.'

'I'm glad too. But you didn't ask me.'

'I did. And you agreed.'

'Not once I found out Jerry wasn't coming.'

The lines she had noticed beside his eyes deepened. 'Is my company so distasteful to you, then?' There was a harsh, demanding intensity in his gaze which it was impossible to evade.

'No, Hal, it's not distasteful. You know that.' Her voice was very quiet and steady.

'Good.' His hand reached out to cradle the back of her head, and Belinda held her breath because his nearness and his potent virility were doing odd things to her heartbeat.

'Then you'll come out with me again, Belinda?'

She nodded, but he didn't take his hand from her hair.

'And you'll dance with me?' Now his voice issued an ultimatum, and she knew that if she didn't take him up on it, but continued to play the mouse, today would be the last day she ever spent with this man. Because he wouldn't let her run away from herself any longer.

'But . . .' she began.

'No buts, Belinda.' Steel and iron, and no evasions.

She took a long breath. 'All right. I'll dance with you.' She stared fixedly into the water. 'I've never been to a charity ball before.'

Hal shook his head as he moved his hand down to circle the back of her neck. 'You're off the hook on that one. I've made other arrangements.'

'Oh—then . . .?'

'I thought, since charity balls weren't your style . . .' his lips contorted briefly '. . . that perhaps you might prefer something more homespun. Mrs Barclay has press-ganged me into buying tickets to the community hall hop for the weekend after next.'

'Oh. I wouldn't have thought community hall hops were *your* style.'

'They're not,' he said grimly, 'but as Mrs Barclay provides most of my lunches and was threatening arsenic, the hop seemed the lesser of two evils.'

Belinda chuckled. 'Mrs Barclay can be very persuasive, can't she?'

'That's one way of putting it, I suppose. Mrs Barclay would have been an asset to the Inquisition.'

'You mean anyone who can sell you a ticket you don't want must be good at extracting confessions?'

'Something like that.'

Belinda didn't believe him. Instinctively she knew he had bought the tickets because he thought she might not be as intimidated by a local dance as she was by a big Vancouver occasion. *Had* she been intimidated? Perhaps, but more by her feelings about Hal than by any society ball.

'So you'll come?'

'Yes.' She could barely get the word out, because now both his hands were behind her back and he was pulling her slowly but quite inescapably into his arms.

When her head came to rest on his shoulder, he bent his neck. And Belinda learned that the lips which she had always thought sensuous were everything she had never allowed herself to imagine.

And much more.

CHAPTER FIVE

AT first Hal's kiss was gentle, as if she were a pale moth whose delicate fragility might crumble at his touch. And at first she stayed still, paralysed by a sensation of such incredible warmth and belonging that she couldn't believe what she had been missing for all these passionless years. Then gradually the warmth changed to heat, and became fire, something hot and scorching that seemed to fuel her whole body with the desire to give all of herself in exchange for all of him. Her arms went around his neck and she parted her lips to receive his tongue. He tasted of burgundy, deep, warm and intoxicating, and his breath was sweet and strong and very male.

His hands moved over her back and then he was pulling her down to lie beside him on the hard, grey rock. He began, a little clumsily, to unbutton her voluminous jacket, and then his fingers were inside it, trailing along her sides, exploring. When the rock began to press into her back, he lifted her so that she was lying across his chest.

Belinda, lost in a sensual world she had never known existed, began to search again for his mouth.

She found it, held her breath, and was just beginning to thrust her fingers into the strong, dark waves of his hair, when she felt something cold and moist touch her neck. Hot, unfragrant breath which she knew had no connection with Hal wafted malodorously across her cheek.

She gasped, rolled away, and sat up.

Two large dogs, one golden and silky, the other black

and scruffy, stood panting happily into Hal's darkly furious face. Then the black one extended an endless pink tongue and began to wash his forehead with damp dedication.

A young boy called from a spot high up on the path above them, and Hal gave vent to a stream of obscenity that would have made Belinda blush—if she had not been so completely fascinated. Even her father, no slouch in that department, had not sworn as impressively as Hal.

'Good dogs. Off you go,' she murmured as the boy called again.

'They are *not* good dogs,' roared Hal, springing to his feet with an agility that made Belinda blink. 'They're bloody interfering, ugly, ill-trained brutes.'

The dogs pricked up their ears, tongues lolling, gave a few more engaging pants and lumbered obligingly up the hill to their master.

'Blasted mutts,' muttered Hal, glaring at the departing backs of the intruders. 'Hairy horrors of doubtful ancestry . . .'

Belinda stared at his glowering, livid face and burst out laughing.

Hal's tirade ceased abruptly. 'I suppose you think that was funny.' His disgruntled expression reminded Belinda of a small boy who had been deprived of a promised treat. She smiled, because in this case the treat had been herself.

'How perceptive of you.' She chuckled, trying hard to contain her amusement.

Hal's lips tightened and he started to raise his arm. Belinda, deciding he needed time to cool off, stood up quickly and began to make her way along the path.

Immediately she felt a firm hand on her elbow.

'Where the hell do you think you're going?'

'Back to the truck. To give you time to cool off.' Honesty seemed the safest course in this situation.'

'Oh, no, you're not.' Before Belinda could answer he had swung her around to face him.

She looked up doubtfully, expecting to see dark eyes still blazing with temper, and that expression of barely controlled fury which made him look so male—and so very sexy.

He did look sexy and male all right. So much so that Belinda felt her heart skip a beat. And his head was still bent at that endearingly belligerent angle—but one corner of his mouth was beginning to quiver and a moment afterwards his lips parted in a rueful, very sheepish grin. Suddenly he put both his arms around her and hugged her against his chest.

'I'm sorry,' he murmured. 'It was funny, wasn't it, when that revolting animal . . .' He paused, shoulders shaking, and then both of them were laughing as they rocked back and forth in each other's arms, consumed with a shared hilarity.

It was in that instant that Belinda knew she was beginning to fall in love.

When they were both exhausted, Hal pulled her to the ground beside him and settled his back against a rock. 'That,' he remarked judicially, 'was a kiss like no other kiss I've ever known—and I *don't* mean just because of the dogs.' He rested his cheek on her hair. 'But then you're a woman like no other woman I've known before, Belinda.'

'Am I?'

Hal saw an odd, strained look in her big eyes now, and was puzzled.

'What is it, love?'

She looked away from him and for a long time didn't answer. When she did, it was to say in a low, almost inaudible voice, 'It's the only kiss I've ever known, Hal.'

'What?' He put his hand on her chin, and turned her face towards him. 'Belinda, don't lie to me. There's no need. Anybody who kisses as you do—like an angel—must have kissed somebody before. And lord knows I've kissed enough women in my life. Don't you know I would never expect you to be what I couldn't be myself?'

She was staring straight into his eyes now. 'All the same, it's true, Hal. You're the first. And probably only,' she added bitterly.

Hal shook his head, his brow furrowing, and Belinda could tell he didn't know whether to believe her or not. In the end he lowered his head from her chin and placed it heavily over her shoulder.

'Why, Belinda?' There was no escaping the question. His eyes demanded an answer.

All right she would tell him. It was only a childish, trivial story of teenage thoughtlessness. All the same, her own immature reaction to it had changed the direction of her life.

'I never had boyfriends when I was going to school,' she began to explain, wishing she could look away from his eyes. 'In fact I only had one close girlfriend. Anthea. She lived at the end of the lane. You see, living on the outskirts of town, I always had to get home to my father after school. He insisted. So there wasn't much time for serious friendships, and anyway I was quiet and not at all pretty, so nobody except Anthea ever bothered with me much. I see more of my schoolmates now than I ever did in those days. Not that I blame anyone for that but myself, because really I've always enjoyed my own company, and I didn't make a lot of effort.'

'That I can believe,' said Hal with feeling.

Belinda's smile came nowhere near her eyes. 'I'm sure you can.'

'All right. Go on.'

When she finally succeeded in looking away from him, she found that it was easier to go on with her gaze fixed hypnotically on the cool, dark waters of the pool.

'So I drifted through school, getting rather good marks because I had nothing to distract me, and then somehow I was in my final year.'

'Graduation year.'

'Yes. Of course nobody asked me to be their partner at the dance and I wasn't even planning to go. Then all of a sudden my father, who had never seemed interested in my social life before—in fact he didn't want me to have one—had . . . an attack of guilt, I suppose. He insisted that I take dancing lessons. So I did. Then he said I had to go to grad. because he didn't want anyone to say it was his fault that his daughter had missed the highlight of her Grade Twelve year. Not that he'd ever cared what anyone thought before. I told him I had no one to go with. But that didn't work, because he knew that the teachers arranged dates for anyone who didn't have a partner. They match names out of a hat, I think. Anyway, once my father had the idea in his head, he was worse than a dog with a bone. He even went out and bought me a dress. It didn't fit, of course, but I've always been good at sewing.'

'I suppose it was a grey one.' Hal's voice, sounding oddly hostile, came from just behind her left ear.

Belinda smiled bleakly. 'It was, as a matter of fact. Dad was quite consistent. He wanted me to go, but he didn't really want me to enjoy myself.'

'Am I right then in assuming that he got his wish?'

'Oh yes. I was paired with Jamie Hansen. He was the shortest boy in the school, with a big nose and poor eyesight. But I didn't mind that. Jamie had always been nice to me, probably because I helped him with his maths, and since I had to go to the dance with someone I hoped we might get along quite well. I mean, he didn't have many friends either. And in those days I was sometimes lonely. I thought it could be fun to go to dances and parties just like everyone else—if anyone ever asked me.'

Almost without her being aware of it, Hal wrapped both arms around her and pulled her head against his chest.

'So what happened?' he asked roughly.

'Oh, Jamie picked me up in a limousine and for once he had a group of friends with him. But not Anthea. She was with the boy she eventually married. Anyway I heard them making remarks about the cottage as soon as they pulled up outside. And they were complaining about the ruts in the lane. I could tell they weren't pleased to have me with them. The girls were all bright and pretty and I spoiled the picture with my plain dress and no make-up. Dad wouldn't let me wear any. Even worse, in those days I was terribly skinny as well—and covered in spots.'

'You don't paint a very alluring portrait of yourself, do you?'

Hal laughed softly, and the sound of his laughter made Belinda go warm inside. Suddenly her graduation night seemed a very long time ago.

'No.' She laughed too. 'I guess I don't. But I think it's accurate. You see, when we got to the dance Jamie refused to dance with me. He spent all evening dancing with Jake Schwartz's date because Jake was having a better time getting drunk. Then, when I came back from hiding in the washroom, I heard Jamie telling Jake's date that he was sure glad he was with her, because otherwise he might have had to dance with me. He said I was the ugliest girl in the whole school and it had been incredible bad luck for him that he'd happened to draw my name.'

Hal said nothing, but his arm tightened imperceptibly on her shoulder.

'I don't think I'd have minded so much if it had been anyone but Jamie,' Belinda went on. 'But he was pretty ugly himself. If I wasn't even good enough for him, then I'd never be good enough for anyone.'

'That little runt needs his butt kicked,' Hal said harshly.

Belinda moved her head in disagreement. 'Not really. He was just young and insecure—like me. And he didn't know how to handle a situation that made him feel awkward.'

'You're much too charitable, Belinda Ballantyne. I'd still like to kick him to Kingdom Come. And do you mean to tell me that, because of that one disastrous evening, you've never gone near a man again?'

She smiled. 'I've gone near lots of them. But not that near. It is true I steered clear of men completely for the first few years after grad—unless they were safely over sixty or under sixteen—but after a while I realised I didn't have a problem. I thought I was keeping them at arm's length but really no one was trying very hard to get close to me—even though by then my spots had gone and I'd put on a bit of weight.' She sighed. 'Of course, apart from my own stand-offishness, my father was a very effective deterrent. A couple of young men did try to get friendly with me when we went into town to do our shopping, but Dad scared them off with his tongue.'

Belinda stared at a soft cloud which momentarily obscured the sun, and then went on quietly, 'Quite honestly, Hal, that was the way I liked it. And now I enjoy my life with my animals, I've got lots to do, I'm not bored and, though I shouldn't say it, since my father died, life has been very peaceful and pleasant.'

'Is that all you want? Peace and pleasantness?' His voice was rough, with an edge to it she didn't understand.

'I suppose so. I have my books and music, I walk and ride my bike. Joe and I go down to Victoria now and then for an art exhibition or a concert. And I do know people in Cinnamon Bay. After all, I've lived here almost all my life. Sometimes I go visiting or to a movie, although of course most of the women my age are married or have high-powered careers in Vancouver or Toronto. But there are still a few of them around to go out with. I'm really quite happy with my life.'

'Are you? Aren't you missing something, Belinda?' In Hal's opinion, Jamie Hansen and this woman's father had a great deal to answer for.

Up until today, Belinda had not been conscious of missing anything. Now she was not so sure.

'Maybe,' she replied slowly. 'I honestly don't know, Hal.'

'Mm.' He moved her forward, stood up and then put his hands under her shoulders to pull her to her feet. For a while he stood behind her, his arms looped over her shoulders and his body moulded against hers. Then, with startling abruptness, he released her and said it was time they got back to the truck.

Belinda, who had been lost in a sensual daze, enjoying his closeness, started, and looked up at the sky. He was right. It was only April, dusk was descending, and it was time to relieve Joe of his charges.

They drove back to Cinnamon Bay in a companionable silence that was very different from the angry atmosphere on the way out, and when Hal helped Belinda down from the truck his hand stayed briefly on her waist. Then it brushed smoothly across her thigh and she shivered. It was an electric, highly charged shiver and immediately he let her go.

He didn't know what to make of this unusual, self-contained young woman who was so different from Dolores, and indeed from any other woman he had known or cared for. Not, he conceded, that he had cared about anyone much since Dolores. He had been careful not to.

He saw lines furrow Belinda's forehead as she looked up at him, and suddenly he was overcome by an urge to smooth away all her worries, to protect her from anything that might hurt her. She was watching his face, wide-eyed and puzzled, and as he stared back, it hit him like a fist in the abdomen that he wanted to do more than protect Belinda. He wanted to possess her, more than he had wanted to possess anyone—or anything—for years. Beautiful Belinda, in the tight jeans and fitted shirt. He had no doubt he could take her too, with very little effort on his part. Probably that had been at the back of his mind all along. Not too far back either. But, he realised, with a sense of incredible frustration, he wasn't going to do it. Not now. Because, for some reason he was only just beginning to understand, he wouldn't be able to live with himself if he hurt her. The knowledge gave him no pleasure. It made him angry.

'I'd better go in now,' she was saying uncertainly. 'Thank you for a beautiful day.'

Hal nodded. 'Yes. I'm glad . . .' He broke off abruptly. 'I have to go away tomorrow, Belinda. I have some business to attend to in Vancouver. But I should be back by the end of next week.'

'Oh.' She looked stunned. 'Oh. But—well, what about your shop?'

'My dear girl,' he replied derisively, 'I didn't build a bicycle empire by putting together every piece of machinery for myself. I may do it occasionally because I happen to enjoy it, but surely you know that running a successful business lies in knowing how to delegate. For goodness sake, Belinda, give me credit for sufficient intelligence to hire competent people to work for me.'

'Yes, of course.' Belinda turned away from him, not wanting him to see that she was fighting to hold back tears. Why was he speaking to her like this? What had she done to make him angry?

But Hal had seen her face as she turned her back, and he knew that his outburst had distressed her. He hadn't intended that. It was just that when he had seen the disappointment on her face because he said he was leaving, he had had enormous difficulty in controlling an urge to reach out and drag her into his arms. And if he did that, he knew he wouldn't be able to let her go. So he had taken refuge in an unkind mockery.

'I didn't mean—I'm sorry—I'll see you next week, Belinda,' he jerked out. Not wanting to, he put out a hand to touch her hair. 'Goodnight.'

Belinda tossed her head away. 'Goodnight,' she replied without looking at him.

A moment later she had disappeared into the house and Hal was left standing alone in the dark.

Damn, he thought, slamming a fist into his palm. Damn. The famous Blake charm had certainly failed to operate this time. He glared at the closed door of cottage, then after a while he shrugged and swung himself up into his truck.

To hell with it. Time enough to worry about this mess—whose name was Belinda Ballantyne—when he came back from Vancouver next week.

'Hah! There you are.' Joe was sitting in the living-room with a salacious eye beamed on a TV movie which, in the quick glimpse Belinda caught before he turned it off, appeared to be baring a great deal of human flesh in intriguingly contorted positions.

'Don't mind me, Joe,' she grinned, her spirits lifting in spite of herself. 'My delicate sensibilities can definitely survive the sight of a bit of skin.'

'Hmph. Lot of rubbish anyway,' huffed Joe, not looking at her. 'Enjoy your afternoon?'

'Not at first.'

At that Joe's lips parted in an approving smirk. 'Served you right, that did, my girl. Hal Blake's my kind of man.'

'In that case,' said Belinda drily, 'I can quite see why you've never been married.'

Joe scowled at her. 'And you'll never marry either, girl, if you don't learn to mind your tongue.'

'I don't intend to.'

'What? Mind your tongue?'

'No, marry, of course.'

'Then you're a damn little fool.'

'You're a fine one to talk.'

Why, Belinda wondered, did she and Joe end up having variations of this conversation almost every time he appeared on her doorstep? It was becoming a continuing source of irritation. If she weren't so fond of the old man . . . But she *was* fond of him. He was part of her life and she didn't know what she would do without him. Deep down, she knew he felt the same about her. In fact they understood each other so well that now, without a word being spoken, both of them decided that it was time to change the subject.

Belinda thanked Joe sincerely for taking care of her menagerie, made him a cup of coffee, and half an hour later watched him shuffle off down the lane after refusing adamantly to let her escort him to his door.

'It's a two-minute walk, girl. I'm not in my dotage yet,' he shouted back at her as he disappeared into the trees.

Belinda smiled and shook her head. No, Joe certainly wasn't in his dotage. Far from it. On the other hand, she mused, as she shut the door behind him, she wasn't exactly a girl either. She was a twenty-six-year-old woman who today had been kissed for the first time. And the man she had been determined to avoid had told her she was almost beautiful.

True, afterwards he had told her he was going away and sneered at her suggesting he couldn't leave his shop—but she was beginning to realise that Hal was much more than the over-confident, overbearing and over-active man she had at first believed him to be. She sighed, and without quite knowing how she had got there, found herself back in the bathroom, staring at her face in the mirror.

Almost beautiful? Had the ugly duckling really turned into a swan? Surely her looks couldn't have improved that much in a few short hours. Once again she studied the small, elfin face with the big luminous eyes. Mm. Perhaps the eyes weren't too bad. There was a light in them now that hadn't been there before. She attempted a smile. Yes, her mouth was too wide, but the smile was not unattractive, and really that turned-up nose was quite—well, neat anyway. And if a man as beautiful as Hal said she was almost beautiful—then maybe, just maybe, it was true.

All right, Belinda, she said to herself now. That's quite enough self-adulation. Vanity will get you nowhere, my girl.

She left the bathroom and made her way into the kitchen, where she found Misty sitting in front of the dog-biscuit cupboard with her nose pointed hopefully at the door.

'You are *not* starving, you know,' said Belinda, giving in and producing the anticipated treat.

Misty flicked the end of her tail and rolled her eyes in the direction of further sustenance.

'Not on your life,' scoffed Belinda. 'Even if I am in a relatively benevolent mood this evening.'

She was, too, in spite of Hal's unkind behaviour just before he had left. She knew instinctively that he hadn't really meant to hurt her. And he had said he would see her next week, so of course he would be back for the community dance.

The dance. Some time soon she would have to ask Joe's advice about a dress. She could make it herself, of course, but he had an artist's eye for design and colour which, as Hal was so fond of pointing out, she hadn't.

And then what? an unwelcome voice whispered in her ear. You'll go to the dance with Hal because you said you would. But you know he's only using you to amuse himself while he's still in Cinnamon Bay. A man as fascinating and successful as Hal Blake is not likely to be seriously interested in Belinda the country mouse—or even in Belinda the porcupine. Soon his business here will be finished and he'll move on to other places—and other, more sophisticated women.

Yes, she thought. That was probably the reason for his derision when he had said goodbye to her. He had been thinking on the way back from the falls, and had come to the conclusion she was an unsophisticated little mouse who was so timid she had never been kissed. She wished now that she hadn't told him that, because she wasn't really as naïve and innocent as he must imagine. She did watch the news, read papers and books, and her world was not entirely bounded by the beaches of Cinnamon Bay.

As she wandered into the bedroom with Misty at her heels, it occurred to her that since saying goodnight to Hal her mood had gone through so many convolutions that she didn't know what she felt any more. Obviously she was quite desperately attracted to him. Maybe—no, not maybe, *definitely* she wanted him to do more than just kiss her. But she didn't want her peaceful life overturned, she didn't want to be hurt again, and even if, by some incredible chance, Hal should ever want a permanent relationship, she knew that on that one score at least her father had been absolutely right.

Look what had happened to poor Anthea. Married at seventeen, divorced at nineteen and left with a child to support. Then married again at twenty-one to an alcoholic who abused her. Now, at last, she was finally pulling her life together after moving to Toronto and starting a career as a social worker. But Anthea swore she would never consider marriage again.

Neither would Belinda. Marriage was a snare that could destroy even the tenuous relationship she now shared with Hal. There were other alternatives, of course, but . . .

Slowly she unbuttoned the shirt that wasn't grey and pulled it off. No, marriage wasn't an issue. All she need worry about at the moment was the dance on Saturday week. She could look forward to that, try to enjoy it when it came, and let the future take care of itself.

Although she was not aware of it, by a slightly more complicated process, Belinda had come to precisely the same conclusion that Hal had reached only an hour or so earlier.

She climbed into bed, lay back on the pillows, and, with Misty reclining comfortably on top of her, she stared up into the darkness and dreamed of Hal. She remembered the warmth and hardness of his body, the burgundy taste of his lips, his sexy, seductive smile . . .

And for the first time in years she was lonely.

In the morning, with animals to take care of, food to prepare and a trip into town to pay bills, the loneliness passed off in a flurry of daytime activity. It was replaced by a feeling of euphoria and anticipation. Hal would only be gone a short time, and now she couldn't wait for his return.

The euphoria lasted until the following Monday morning when she opened the paper, spread it on the kitchen table and on the front of the second section saw a half-page photograph of Hal.

He was wearing evening dress, and he looked powerful and magnificent and untouchable, in a way she had never imagined possible when she had seen him in the casual denims he favoured around Cinnamon Bay. His head was slanted sideways, and he was smiling at a tall, willowy brunette who obviously had no reservations about touching him. She was clinging with soft possessiveness to his arm as she gazed adoringly into his face.

Beneath the picture was a caption which read, 'Well-known bicycle importer and philanthropist Hal Blake seen arriving at the Pan-Pacific Hotel with his partner, actress Shelagh Devine. Mr Blake assured reporters there is no truth in the rumour that he and Ms Devine are shortly to announce their engagement.'

CHAPTER SIX

BELINDA'S vision blurred, and Hal's imposing, black-clad figure seemed to sway in front of her eyes. Then suddenly she could see everything quite clearly and the letters of the caption stood out in stark relief against the page.

'Actress Shelagh Devine—no truth in the rumour—announce their engagement.'

No truth? But celebrities, from the Royal Family, to Hollywood stars, to successful businessmen like Hal, always said there was no truth in rumours that were frequently confirmed as fact only a few days later. And there had to be some explanation for the look of proud possession on Shelagh Devine's lovely face. Vaguely, Belinda remembered reading about the luscious Ms Devine. There had been an article in a magazine about Canadian actresses destined for Hollywood stardom—and Hal's clinging partner had been one.

To her bewilderment, Belinda saw a tear splash on to the paper. It was followed by another and another as gradually the actress's face became smudged and wet and bloated. She dashed the back of her hand across her eyes. This was ridiculous. She rarely cried, and she wasn't going to start now just because Hal had gone to the ball at the Pan-Pacific with Shelagh Devine. He had a right to go with anyone he pleased. After all, she had turned him down herself.

Yes, she thought sourly, and it hadn't taken him long to find a replacement. A particularly gorgeous replacement. It was odd, though . . . If Hal was soon to be engaged to Ms Devine, why had he asked her, Belinda, in the first place?

The question continued to gnaw at her for the rest of the morning, providing a kind of comfort, and it was only when Mr and Mrs Jellicoe arrived from the town with a spitting, unhappy black cat that it came to her that of course Hal and Shelagh had probably had a quarrel, which had been made up the moment he called to ask her to the ball. No wonder the actress was looking so smug and soft—just as Belinda's new boarder, after he had been given food and milk and a comfortable bed began to lick his paws and look complacent.

Yes, of course that was it. Hal and his girlfriend had made up their differences, and now that hostilities were over the engagement would probably be announced any day—whatever Hal might have said when he was cornered by a bunch of nosy reporters. And that, she told herself dully, puts an end to all those childish dreams about the Cinnamon Bay community hop. Because of course Hal wouldn't be taking her now. When—if—he came back to the Island, he would explain that the invitation had been an unfortunate mistake.

Oh, that knowledge put an end to dreams all right—and to euphoria and excitement and decisions about new dresses. And much as she tried to convince herself it didn't matter, that she was glad to resume her even, uneventful life, in the end she was forced to admit that her life was not just even and uneventful. It was dull. It was empty. And she missed Hal terribly. She had a frightening presentiment that from now on she always would, because she had lost her taste for solitude and stubborn independence. In fact she was beginning to think her love of privacy had only been an attitude she had adopted to hide her real needs from herself.

'Rubbish,' said Joe, when Belinda told him about the picture. 'If Hal Blake said he'd take you to that dance, then he will.'

'No.' Belinda shook her head. 'It wouldn't be fair to Shelagh.'

'Rubbish,' Joe said again, pounding his gnarled fist on her table. 'I saw that picture too, and if ever I saw a piece of useless baggage, that Shelagh Devine has to be it. OK, so he needed a partner at some dance. So what? You told me yourself you turned him down. Silly little fool. But he'll be back. That young man has more sense than you give him credit for, Bella. Now—you get yourself a pretty dress picked out for him and let's have no more nonsense.'

'No, Joe. What's the use?'

'Use! I'll tell you what's the use, you blind little . . .'

'I know. Fool,' sighed Belinda. 'Well, I may be a fool, but I'm not doing anything about a dress that I'll never even have a chance to wear.'

'Obstinate female donkey,' Joe shouted. Then he turned his back on her, stomped out of the kitchen and slammed the door.

Joe had done a lot of door-slamming lately, Belinda reflected. Ever since Hal had come on the scene, it seemed. Well, he could slam all the doors he liked, she still wasn't getting a dress.

Late on Friday night the phone rang. Belinda was just preparing for bed and her mouth was full of toothpaste when she picked up the receiver and said curtly, 'Yes. Who is it?'

There was silence for a moment and then Hal's deep, resonant voice said softly, 'This must be the porcupine residence. Have I called at a bad time?'

Belinda felt her heart bump down to her feet and then

surge up again to hammer suffocatingly at her chest.

'Belinda, are you there?'

'No,' she gasped idiotically, as the toothpaste oozed down her throat.

'Ah. I thought not.' From the slight sharpness in his tone she couldn't tell if he was amused or impatient.

'I mean—yes, I'm here. But why are you?'

'Why am I what?'

'Here.'

Belinda knew that if she could see him right now, Hal would be leaning heavily against a wall and either closing his eyes in disgust or raising them in resigned exasperation to the ceiling.

'Because I said I would be. Belinda, have you gone out of your mind?' Obviously exasperation had won the day.

'No,' she replied stonily.

'Oh. Then perhaps you're suffering from loss of memory.' The sharpness in his voice was honed to a very fine edge.

'There's nothing the matter with my memory.'

'In that case you'll recall that we have a date for tomorrow night, Miss Ballantyne.'

Miss Ballantyne indeed. He hadn't called her that since that first day in his bicycle shop.

'We had,' she replied stiffly. 'But I presumed it's been cancelled.'

'Why should you presume that?' His voice was as stiff as hers, but harder.

'Because—because I saw that picture in the paper, Hal. You're engaged to Shelagh Devine.'

Belinda had already discovered that Hal had a distinctive vocabulary. Now, as she held the phone away from her ear, she discovered just how far its depth and range extended.

She let him go on for a while and then interrupted with genuine anxiety, 'Hal! Hal, stop it. You'll get my phone disconnected.'

She heard him breathing heavily for a moment and then his voice roared over the wires at her, 'If I do, it will damn well serve you right, you impossible woman.'

Why were people always telling her things served her right? Was she that hard to get along with?

She asked him. 'Why? Why will it serve me right?'

Hal swore again. 'Belinda—Belinda, are you *sure* you're not out of your mind?'

'Quite sure.'

'Then what the hell do you mean by suggesting I'm engaged to Shelagh? Can't you read? I told those reporters they were talking a load of—baloney.'

'I know. But she looked so adoring. And people always say that.'

'Oh, do they? Well, I don't. And Shelagh's an actress. She's paid to look adoring. I am not engaged to her, I never have been, and I never will be. She's the daughter of an old friend of my father's. *We're* friends. She's a good actress with the body of a goddess and the brains of a chicken, and she thinks I'm a boring older man with a child. But we do each other favours on occasion, and she happened to be free on Saturday night. In view of the fact that you turned me down, Belinda, I don't think you have any right to object.'

No, of course she hadn't. No right at all. Hal had made her no promises, nor had she asked for any. And he had probably had no choice about attending the ball. Not after he had made a commitment. She should be thankful he hadn't asked someone who wasn't the chicken-brained daughter of his father's friend.

'You're right,' she agreed in a very small voice. 'I'm sorry, Hal. Thank you for calling me.'

'That's better. I hope you're properly chastened. If not, I'll see to it when I come to pick you up tomorrow—at about six-thirty. We'll have dinner at the Inn before the dance.'

'Yes, Hal.' He didn't sound in any mood for argument. Anyway she didn't want to argue any more.

Misty, seeing the blissful smile on her mistress's face, headed purposefully in the direction of her biscuits. Obligingly, Belinda produced the required treat without even taking in the fact that she had been conned.

The following morning she awoke with the knowledge that something wonderful had happened, and a few seconds later she recalled that the something was Hal. She beamed happily up at the ceiling and shifted Misty gently off her stomach.

And then it hit her.

She couldn't possibly go to the dance tonight because she didn't have anything to wear.

Frantically her mind ran over the contents of her wardrobe. Jeans, jogging-suits and two printed skirts for special occasions. Nothing that was remotely suitable for dancing, not even for the community hop. Help! Was there anything possible in the attic? Her old graduation dress wouldn't fit, but perhaps there was something of her mother's . . .

She was just making breakfast after a dusty reconnaissance of the attic, when the telephone rang.

'Bella? Blake's back. Did he call you?'

'Yes. Yes, he did, Joe. You were right. But—oh, Joe, you *were* right. I haven't got anything to wear. At least—I did find an old beige dress of my mother's. Dad must have kept it. I suppose that wouldn't do, would it?'

This lovely Victorian pewter-finish miniature is perfect for displaying a treasured photograph. And it's yours FREE as added thanks for giving our Reader Service a try!

Harlequin Reader Service® Sweepstakes Entry Form

This is your **unique** Sweepstakes Entry Number: 1U 943516

This could be your lucky day! If you have the winning number, you could be the Grand Prize Winner. To be eligible, *affix Sweepstakes Entry Sticker here!* (SEE OFFICIAL SWEEPSTAKES RULES IN BACK OF BOOK FOR DETAILS).

If you would like a chance to win the $25,000.00 prize, the $10,000.00 prize, or one of the many $5,000.00, $1,000.00, $250.00 or $10.00 prizes…plus the Mustang and the Hawaiian Vacation, *affix Prize Sticker here!*

To receive free books and gifts with no obligation to buy, as explained on the opposite page, *affix the Free Books and Gifts Sticker here!*

Please enter me in the sweepstakes and, when the winner is drawn, tell me if I've won the $1,000,000.00 Grand Prize! Also tell me if I've won any other prize, including the car and the vacation prize. Please ship me the free books and gifts I've requested with sticker above. Entering the Sweepstakes costs me nothing and places me under no obligation to buy! (If you do not wish to receive free books and gifts, do not affix the FREE BOOKS and GIFTS sticker.)

306 CIH ACH2
(C-H-P-04/91)

YOUR NAME PLEASE PRINT

ADDRESS APT#

CITY PROVINCE POSTAL CODE

Offer limited to one per household and not valid for current Harlequin Presents® subscribers.

Printed in U.S.A.

DETACH AND MAIL TODAY!

Harlequin's "No Risk" Guarantee

- You're not required to buy a single book—ever!
- As a subscriber, you must be completely satisfied or you may cancel at any time by marking "cancel" on your statement or returning a shipment of books at our cost.
- The free books and gifts you receive are yours to keep.

If card is missing, write to: Harlequin Reader Service, P.O. Box 609,
Fort Erie, Ontario L2A 5X3

Printed in U.S.A.

Business Reply Mail
No Postage Stamp
Necessary if Mailed
in Canada
Postage will be paid by

HARLEQUIN READER SERVICE®
P.O. BOX 609
FORT ERIE, ONTARIO
L2A 9Z9

'It would not. Beige indeed. Your mother was a redhead, Bella. She looked a dream in beige. You, girl, on the other hand, would look like a cup of cold tea.'

'Thanks. You and Hal are so good for my morale.'

'That's your fault.'

'Maybe. Anyway, I guess that means I won't be able to go.'

'Nonsense. It's Saturday. There are at least three dress shops open in the town today.'

'Yes, but . . .'

'And don't you "but" me. I'll be over in half an hour. You and I are going shopping.'

Joe hung up the phone without waiting for an answer, and half an hour later to the minute he was stamping up the path to her door.

Belinda watched him coming. Dear, gruff, crusty old Joe, who despite all his rough edges painted the most beautiful pictures, and had the kindest heart of anyone she knew.

'You don't have to bother, Joe,' she told him as he approached her. 'I can easily pick out something for myself.'

'Oh, no, you don't, my girl. I know what you'll come home with. Some awful confection in beige and grey.'

Belinda had been thinking of navy blue, but she didn't say so.

When they arrived at the nearest dress shop its owner, Mrs Alcott bustled out from behind the counter with her mouth open in a startled smile. 'Belinda! I haven't seen you in months. Come to pick up some more T-shirts, have you dear? Hello, Mr MacIlwain, and how are you today?'

'Same as I was yesterday,' growled Joe. 'And she has *not* come to pick up T-shirts, she's come to buy a dress.'

'A navy blue one, I think,' said Belinda hastily. 'Or maybe black.'

'Forget it.' Joe's irascible bark caused two young women on their way into the shop to change their minds and head for the competition. Mrs Alcott gave him a repressive glare and asked him to keep his voice down.

'All right, you find something young and bright for Belinda here, and I won't say another word.'

'That'll be the day,' muttered Belinda under her breath.

As it turned out, Joe said a lot of words, in short order rejecting a black wool, two navy blue and white linens and something brown and synthetic. Then Mrs Alcott produced a stunning three-quarter-length dress made of rippling royal blue silk, and Joe said, 'Fine. That's it.'

'Oh, I don't know . . .' began Belinda.

'Well, I do. Try it on.'

It was easier to do as Joe wished than to argue, and when she saw her reflection in the long changing-room mirror she could hardly believe what she saw. The rich, glowing colour brought out the lights in her eyes and gave her pale complexion a warm, inner glow of its own. The low-cut bodice with short cap sleeves ended just below her waist and from there the skirt flowed softly out over her hips to accentuate every curve of her slender figure.

'Oh, you look an absolute vision,' gushed Mrs Alcott. 'I wouldn't have believed it possible.'

Joe's eyes, under the beetling brows, were suspiciously moist.

'We'll take it,' he said abruptly.

'I'll take it,' smiled Belinda, when she saw that he was about to write a cheque. 'I can easily afford it, Joe.'

The ensuing argument only ended when Belinda

agreed to let him buy her a pair of silver shoes—for her birthday which was not until November.

That evening, as she slipped the dress over her head, and for the first time in her life took the trouble to apply a little make-up, she remembered Mrs Alcott's unflattering comment that she wouldn't have believed it possible. Belinda found she was inclined to agree. She barely recognised the attractive—almost beautiful?—young woman who was smiling back at her from the glass.

She glanced at her watch. Only six o'clock. Young Jack Oliphant, who was coming to look after the animals because Joe was an early riser and she didn't want to keep him up, wasn't due for another fifteen minutes. She wandered into the living-room and turned on Prokofiev's *Romeo and Juliet.*

It was not until many hours later that it occurred to her that her choice of music might have been an unconscious foreknowledge of shadows which were yet to fall.

The sonorous strains of 'The End of Tybalt' were fading into the air as Belinda finished telling Jack about the care and feeding of her furry and scaly house-guests. She was so absorbed in emphasising that the Jellicoes' black cat was not, under any circumstances, to be permitted near little Jimmy Smith's white mice, that she didn't hear the impatient rap on the door.

A moment later it swung open and the kitchen seemed suddenly smaller, and overpoweringly full of Hal.

'You ought to keep you door locked, Belinda. It's asking for trouble to leave it open like that. Especially when you can't hear a thing above that racket.'

Yes, that was Hal, all right.

Belinda, who had been leaning over the mouse cage,

straightened slowly. He was standing just inside the door with his arms crossed, looking expensive and domineering in a beautifully tailored dark suit. Immediately she felt a familiar tug of desire, followed by an equally familiar surge of irritation.

'It's not a racket and I'm not asking for trouble,' she snapped disagreeably. 'What on earth could possibly happen to me out there?'

But Hal's eyes had widened as they swept approvingly over her figure, taking in the blue dress, the touch of colour in her cheeks and the indignant sparkle in her eyes, and he didn't respond at once. When he did, it was to say in a voice which had thickened slightly, 'If you want an answer to that, you little idiot, just go and look in the mirror.'

'What? What do you mean?'

For answer, Hal took one stride across the room, caught her by the shoulders, turned her around and propelled her into the bedroom. Behind him young Jack stood with his mouth open and his eyes alight with vicarious anticipation.

'Look at yourself,' said Hal, marching her up to the long mirror which hung on the wall beside her bed.

Belinda looked. 'Well?'

'What do you see?'

'I see a—a woman in a royal blue dress. With a dark man standing behind her looking disgustingly bossy.'

She also saw the fingers of the dark man's hands begin to slide up her neck until they were cupping the back of her head and pushing up under her hair.

'You need someone to be disgustingly bossy, young lady. Can you imagine what would happen if some stranger came wandering through your unlocked door and saw you looking like that?'

'Like what?'

'Like a luscious, desirable little plum just waiting to be plucked. Good heavens, Belinda, I told you you shouldn't wear grey, but I had no idea . . .' He broke off and his firm hands pressed over her shoulders, down sides and then slowly, deliriously, around her hips, pulling her back against his body.

Belinda gasped and stared at his set face in the glass.

'Hell,' muttered Hal. 'Let's get out of here, woman, or it won't by any stranger you'll need to beware of. It'll be me.'

'I'm not frightened of you, Hal.'

'Well, you ought to be,' he said grimly. 'Come on.' As peremptorily as he had marched into the bedroom, he now marched out again, in the process almost bowling over young Jack, who was peering through the half-open door.

A few minutes later they were speeding down the lane in what to Belinda's incredulous eyes looked remarkably like a Mercedes.

'What happened to your truck?' she asked dazedly. 'Why aren't you driving it tonight?'

'Oh, come on, Belinda. Surely you didn't expect me to drive *you*, looking like a million dollars, in one of Blake's company trucks—looking like exactly what it is.'

He sounded so scathing and superior that Belinda felt defensive.

Did he really think he could talk to her as if she were a congenital fool just because he happened to have praised her appearance? If that was the case, she was going right back to grey.

'I don't know what I expected,' she replied haughtily. 'Certainly not a Mercedes.'

'Does it impress you?' His head slanted sideways and the smile he gave her was full of amused affection—and quite maddeningly attractive.

'No,' lied Belinda.

Hal went on smiling his superior smile, and, although she no longer really believed he meant to mock her, by the time they arrived at the Inn on the Beach Belinda was ready to kick him. She changed her mind though when he helped her out of the car and put his arm around her waist to lead her into the Inn. With his hard body warm and strong against hers, she found that all she truly wanted to do was kiss him.

They were shown to a secluded table by a large picture window overlooking the sea, and the head waiter, who knew Belinda by sight because she occasionally came here with Joe, raised his eyebrows in surprised approval when he saw who her escort was tonight.

Hal, who seemed to have it firmly fixed in his head that she needed looking after, ordered for both of them, and to her surprise she found she didn't mind. It made a change from making all her own decisions, as she had had to do ever since her father died. Just as long as Hal didn't get the idea that he had a right to organise her life. She had no doubt whatever that given half a chance he would try. She had seen enough of the masterful Mr Blake to know that he expected the world to do his bidding.

She smiled, a little, secret smile. If Hal thought he could organise her, then he had another think coming.

'Why the sly smirk, Belinda?' asked Hal as their salads arrived.

'What smirk? I never smirk,' she said quickly.

'Is that so? Then why does that *smile* I just saw on

your face give me the definite impression that you have something unpleasant in store—for me, presumably.'

'Not at all,' laughed Belinda. 'If you really want to know, I was just deciding that, although you're welcome to order my dinner, you're not ordering anything else.'

Hal raised his eyebrows. 'Such as?'

'Oh, I don't know.' Suddenly she felt confused and a little presumptuous. After all, what, besides food, could he possibly want to order?

She soon found out. Half-way through the beautifully tender roast beef—somehow she had suspected Hal would be a meat and potatoes man—he informed her that he was sending over a new bicycle for her in the morning.

'That heap of yours is no good for anything,' he announced bluntly. 'What you need is a nice light racing-bike.'

'I do not. I don't race. And I'm fond of my old bike.'

'It's a piece of junk. All right, I'll send you a touring-bike then. How about a Miyata? Or a Trek?'

'Hal, no. I'm quite happy with what I have. Why can't you leave it at that?'

He smiled, a warm, tender smile that lit up his eyes. 'Don't you understand, love? I want to give you something.'

'But . . .'

'No, don't interrupt. You're such an independent little porcupine that I couldn't think of anything else you'd accept. Tell me, what would you say if I bought you a diamond bracelet?'

Just like that. As if a diamond bracelet were an everyday affair—like some tawdry piece of paste from a street stall. 'I'd give it back,' she replied without hesitation.

He shrugged. 'You see. That's why I decided on the bike. They're my business, I have a store full of them, and I thought that for once you might manage to accept something from me graciously.' He lowered his heavy lids so that she couldn't see his eyes, and added, 'There's nothing very compromising about a bike.'

'Compromising?'

'Jewellery is often offered in the expectation of certain—hm—services, in return,' he explained drily.

'I know,' said Belinda, wondering if he really thought she was as naïve as all that. Now he was studying her with an intense, speculative gaze that made her uneasy. All right, she would accept the bike—graciously—and change the subject.

When she thanked him politely and said that she'd be delighted to have a new bike, Hal looked so male and triumphant that she almost withdrew her acceptance. She would have done precisely that if she hadn't had a strong suspicion that he would deliver the bike anyway—probably broken explosively over her head.

'What started you in the bicycle business?' she asked hastily, carrying out her plan to change the subject.

It proved a fortunate topic and she was genuinely interested, Hal gave her an eloquent description of his beginnings in the bike trade. Apparently he had started by exchanging the profits from some unexpected successes on the stock market for his first small shop in Victoria. From that modest purchase had grown a bicycle empire which, Belinda guessed, now turned over millions of dollars a year.

'It must keep you incredibly busy,' she remarked thoughtfully when he had finished. 'No wonder you don't have much time for Jerry.'

Hal's eyes deepened and his face seemed to darken slowly. 'Yes,' he said without inflection. 'Jerry can be a problem.' He picked up a knife and cut viciously into his meat. 'I don't like to admit it, Belinda, but sometimes I think my mother has to be right. Jerry and I should have a permanent home of our own somewhere. In Victoria, I suppose.'

'Is that where your head office is?'

'Yes.' Now he was staring through the window at the grey, storm-tossed waves. Funny, it hadn't even been raining when they arrived.

'But your mother's home? That's permanent, isn't it? Couldn't you spend more time there?'

Hal gave a short, hard laugh. 'You haven't tried living with my mother, have you? She has eyes like a hawk, a tongue to match, an opinion on every subject under the sun, which she doesn't hesitate to express—until in the end she's either got you agreeing with her, or else driven you out of the house.'

'I expect she worries about you.'

'Oh, she does that all right,' he agreed gloomily.

'Then why not make her—and Jerry—happy? You could buy a house in Victoria and run the business from there. You don't actually have to go away so often, do you?'

'You and my mother would get on like a house on fire,' said Hal unpleasantly. Then, seeing her stricken face, he added quickly, 'I'm sorry. I didn't mean to bite your head off. It's just that it never seems to occur to anyone . . .'

'That you're too restless to settle down in one place because you're also too lonely,' said Belinda with a flash of understanding.

'I'm not in the least lonely. Alone, yes. But that's not

the same thing, is it? And for your information, I have a perfectly satisfactory flat in Victoria which I use on those occasions when I want—privacy. So I hardly need another house, do I?' He was still staring out at the sea, and Belinda had no illusions as to the reasons why a man like Hal might want privacy.

'You miss your wife, don't you?' she said gently. Although she knew he would probably resent the question, she still felt it had to be asked.

The look he threw her now was filled with scorn. She hadn't thought his hot, dark eyes could look so cruel. 'No,' he said bleakly. 'I don't miss my—Dolores. Any more than she misses her son.' His fingers clenched so tightly around the stem of his wine glass that Belinda was afraid he would break it. But somehow she knew his anger was not really directed at her.

'Dolores left us when Jerry was two years old. I was making money by then, but not nearly enough for her. She told me she was bored and that old Bugattis were more her style than new bicycles.' He gave a laugh in which there was not hint of amusement. 'The fact is, Dolores is incapable of love. She hasn't seen Jerry once since the day she left.'

'Do you know where she is?' asked Belinda quietly.

'Not exactly. Last heard of on the French Riviera with a count who owns a priceless collection of cars.'

'I thought counts were always penniless these days.'

Not this one. Although no doubt he soon will be. Dolores will see to that.' He slammed his fist down on the table, making the glasses rattle, and impulsively Belinda reached across the table and covered his bunched knuckles with her hand.

Hal looked up and gave her brief, mirthless smile. 'I'm sorry, beautiful Belinda.' He put his other hand over hers, trapping her small fingers between his big ones. 'And now that we've finished dissecting my less than fascinating past, why don't you tell me about yours? Why did you and your father hide yourselves away in the bush all those years? And why are *you* still doing it?'

'I've told you about me. I'm doing what I want to do. As for my father—that's another story.'

'Tell me.'

He was still holding fast to her hand, and odd little tremors were running up her arm as his eyes seemed to bore into her skull. She didn't really want to talk about the sour, embittered man her father had become after he gave up prospecting in the North to marry her mother—with whom he had been living off and on for years—and then, discovering that marriage had destroyed his affection, left her for his cottage in the woods—along with the infant daughter his wife no longer wanted.

She and Jerry had a lot in common, she realised, as Hal waited for her to continue, and she found it was impossible not to do as he asked. If he wanted to know about her father, she would tell him. He had an uncanny ability to make her do what he wanted, and it was an ability she was not at all sure she appreciated.

All the same, as briefly as possible, she explained about her father.

'So now we know all there is to know about each other,' said Hal softly when she had finished. 'Poor little porcupine.'

'I'm not poor. Or a porcupine.' She smiled shakily.

'No, maybe you're not.' He put his hand gently beneath his chin. 'Do you think then that perhaps we should both leave our shadows in the past—where they belong?'

'Yes,' agreed Belinda. 'Yes, let's leave them.' But in her heart she knew that Hal had not told her everything and that the shadows could not remain hidden forever.

The wind had come up with a vengeance by the time they left the Inn, and the waves were pounding on the beach with a dull and persistent roar. Even with the thin coat Belinda had brought to wear over her dress, she was chilled to the bone by the time they got into the car.

'You looked like a drowned rat,' laughed Hal, as he turned to look at her. 'Your hair is all plastered to your head.' When he saw the look of distress in her big eyes, he added quickly, 'A very beautiful little rat, though.' Smiling, he leaned across, put his hands inside her coat and kissed her.

Belinda, who had spent over a week trying to forget his kisses, responded in a way that left Hal breathing hard, and leaning heavily away from her against the door.

'I thought you told me you had no experience,' he said huskily, wiping a handkerchief across his forehead to remove moisture that was by no means all caused by the rain.

Belinda turned her eyes to the sea. 'I think some things are instinctive,' she said shyly. She might look like a drowned rat, but had he any idea what he did to her, all dark and sexy and smiling, with his hair shining wetly on his face?

Obviously he hadn't, because now he straightened, patted her thigh in a gesture of casual possessiveness which left her reeling, and started the engine of the car.

The music from a lively band was spilling out into the street when they arrived at the Community Hall. So were a number of the dancers. April had passed, it was the beginning of May, and now that they were away from the winds and waves of the beach the air was surprisingly warm.

'The rain must have stopped,' said Belinda with relief, as Hal parked his Mercedes in the car park, surreptitiously watched by a small crowd of revellers who had suddenly found it expedient to shuffle his way.

'It has,' said Hal, helping her out. 'You'll be dry by the time you've combed your hair.'

She didn't tell him he ought to comb his too, because she liked it the way it was, all waving and windblown about his face.

By the time she emerged from the ladies' room, with her hair and face restored, Hal was already surrounded by a crowd. It was headed by Mrs Barclay, who was introducing him to the assembled company as if he were her own personal triumph—which in a way he was, conceded Belinda wryly, as she tried to push her way to his side.

'What do you think of our decorations, Mr Blake?' Mrs Barclay was trilling, as Hal extended a hand to pull Belinda to him past two entranced schoolgirls and a man in a startlingly green tartan suit.

'Mm. Very—er—very decorative,' said Hal, casting a wary eye over the colourful crêpe streamers and bedraggled paper flowers, half of which had already fallen to the floor, while the rest clung precariously to the sticky tape which was supposed to hold them in place.

'Humbug,' whispered Belinda out of the corner of her mouth.

'Porcupine,' Hal murmured back out of his.

Then they both straightened guiltily as Mrs Barclay fixed them with a beady eye and said reprovingly, 'Our

Ladies' Committee spent a lot of time and trouble decorating this hall. I hope you appreciate that, Belinda.'

So Hal was going to get away with what amounted to unseemly disrespect for the Ladies' Committee, while she, Belinda, was unfairly expected to shoulder all the blame.

'Oh, I do, Mrs Barclay,' she replied with wide-eyed innocence. 'I think the flowers on the floor are a perfectly lovely idea.'

Beside her, she heard Hal choke into a glass of beer. 'I'll get you a drink, Belinda,' he muttered quickly, wending his way through the crowd with a few Houdini-like twists which left Belinda gaping with admiration—and Mrs Barclay scowling in frustration.

'Well,' said the irate hostess, turning back to Belinda. 'We haven't seen you here before, have we, miss? But then I suppose we don't normally provide sufficiently impressive partners to attract you.'

She cast a sour look at Hal's retreating back, and Belinda wondered what she could have done to bring down all this venom on her head. Mrs Barclay was a gossip who knew everyone's business, but she wasn't usually deliberately unkind. Then a tall, ginger-haired girl with a big nose walked up to Hal as he hoisted a drink from the bar, and things suddenly fell into place. Of course. Mrs Barclay had been trying to marry off her daughter Margaret for years, and in a town like Cinnamon Bay the eligible male pickings were pretty slim. Besides, even in a good year, Hal would stand out head and shoulders above the rest, in every sense.

But now Mrs Barclay's mouth narrowed as she saw Hal brush Margaret off with a polite nod, and make his way back to Belinda.

She had only taken one sip of the drink he brought her when the man in green tartan, after a quick nudge from Mrs Barclay, pushed past Hal and demanded the next dance.

Oh, dear. She hadn't even danced with Hal yet. She glanced up at him enquiringly, but apart from an enigmatic little smile his expression was unhelpfully blank.

'Er—thank you,' she replied, to the man she was beginning to label 'the green man'. She placed her drink on a table and stepped reluctantly into his arms.

Immediately he pulled her much to close, but as the band was playing something slow and sensual there was no way she could tactfully shove him off. When she looked around for Hal, he was dancing with Margaret Barclay. Like the green man, he was holding Margaret much too close, and Belinda noted with a shock of emotion which she was horrified to recognise as jealousy that he was moving with a raw subconscious sexuality that made her want to tear herself from her partner's arms and hurl herself into Hal's.

Then the music changed, became faster, louder and more rhythmic. The green man swung Belinda away from him and began to gyrate in front of her in a way which she supposed he imagined was seductive. In fact it only made her want to laugh. Hal, she noticed, was also gyrating, but his movements weren't funny at all. They were sensuous, erotic and hypnotic, and her eyes were riveted on his hips and thighs as they twisted sinuously under the dim and flickering lights. Then he raised his arms slowly above his head and began to revolve around Margaret in a manner that was so suggestive that Mrs Barclay, with a cry of indignation that was audible all over the hall, pushed her way across the floor, grabbed Margaret by the hand and hauled her away from Hal towards the cloakroom.

Hal, with a grin of pure devilment, stopped dancing, strode over to Belinda, and with a murmured and very final 'excuse me' to the green man, swung her imperiously into his arms.

'You should be ashamed of yourself, Hal,' she told him, trying to sound disapproving. 'That was a disgraceful exhibition, and you know it.'

'Mm,' he murmured smugly into her hair. 'Of course I know it. But it worked. I'll no longer get Margaret Barclay served up for breakfast, lunch and dinner every time I decide to eat at the café.' He sighed. 'On the other hand, I'll very likely get arsenic in my coffee.'

'Serve you right,' retorted Belinda, delighted that for once those words came from her lips instead of his.

For answer Hal slid both arms down her back and began to rotate a thumb slowly and intoxicatingly around the base of her spine.

With difficulty, Belinda stopped herself from arching against him. 'Don't,' she gasped. 'You'll ruin my reputation.'

'Do you mind?'

'No,' she groaned, as his thumb continued to do impossible things to her nerve-ends. 'No, Hal, I don't think I mind at all.'

'Good. Then let's get out of here so I can ruin your reputation properly—somewhere private.'

For a moment Belinda stood stock still, staring up at his wickedly smiling face. Then, with her eyes fixed on his, she nodded. 'Yes,' she whispered, so softly that only he could hear her. 'Yes, Hal. Please let's.'

CHAPTER SEVEN

HAL drove rather too fast through the empty, moonlit streets and both of them were silent until they pulled into the driveway of a large bungalow set in spacious grounds in the town's most affluent residential section. They were still silent as Hal inserted a key in the lock and, with his hand on the small of her back, urged Belinda gently inside. Inevitably, he slammed the door shut behind them.

She glanced curiously around the room and then said quietly, 'It's exactly the way I thought your house would be.'

'Is it?' The smile he gave her was both amused and sceptical. 'I didn't know I was quite so predictable.'

'You're not. But you are very—well, *masculine*.'

'I'm glad to hear it. Not that I entirely see what my gender has to do with my house.'

'It has everything to do with it,' she said appreciatively. 'I knew you would have thick-pile carpets and teak bookcases—and lots of lovely, supple black leather.'

Hal arched an eyebrow at her and grinned. 'Supple black leather? I'm not sure I like the sound of that. What did you have in mind exactly?'

Belinda laughed and refused to rise to the bait. 'Not what you seem to think.' She looked away from him and let her eyes roam along the smooth, ivory-white walls. 'Not too many holes, I see,' she remarked idly. 'Unless you count the ones you had to make to hang your Indian carvings. You have some fascinating pieces, Hal.'

'Yes.' His eyes followed hers and lit with the immediate enthusiasm of the collector. 'I'm glad you feel the same way about them as I do.' He looped his arm around her shoulder and they stood side by side, lost in admiration of the art—and of each other.

Then gradually a guarded look passed over Hal's face as he asked in a tone suddenly gone wary, 'Holes, Belinda? Did you say not too many *holes*?'

'Yes, I did.' Belinda regarded him gravely, but her big dark eyes were dancing. 'Joe says you always buy your houses instead of renting—so that you can put holes in the walls.'

'Your friend Joe must have a very odd opinion of me.' His mouth twisted quizzically. 'Why would I want holes in the wall?'

'I suppose he meant for pictures. Unless . . .' She grinned mischievously. 'Unless he thinks you're in the habit of putting your fist through them to relieve your frustrations when you happen to have had a bad day.'

'Not as a general rule,' he replied drily. 'I have been tempted on occasions, I must admit, but I have other ways of relieving my—frustrations.'

He was looking at her with a sort of teasing challenge in his eye, and for a moment she wondered what she was doing here, alone, in this house, with a man who was tempted to put fists through walls and who could make her lose all sense of direction with just one glance from his gleaming, velvet-dark eyes.

'Are—are you going to sell this house again soon?' she asked in a voice which she knew had risen unnaturally high. Suddenly she needed this conversation to be ordinary, down to earth—and preferably rather dull.

Then she realised she didn't want to hear his answer

because it might be 'yes'.

'Do you think I should?'

Belinda saw from the way his jaw had tightened that in her efforts to reduce everything to the ordinary, she had managed to ask precisely the wrong question. 'No,' she replied quickly. 'At least, I mean that's up to you, I guess.'

'It is, isn't it?' he replied evenly. His features relaxed. 'Meanwhile, I'm glad you like it.'

'Oh, I do. It's beautiful. I love it.'

And she did. The wall-to-wall white carpet added to the feeling of spaciousness, and the low black couches and padded armchairs provided a stark and attractive contrast to the polished warmth of the teak. But above all, everything in the room, from the coolly smooth Inuit ornaments to the Indian carvings and the books on bicycles, baseball and business, was imbued with the feel and the flavour of Hal.

She looked up at him and smiled hesitantly, overcome by a surprising shyness. What was she doing here in this house which was so obviously Hal's, waiting—waiting for what?

Hal, seeing the doubt in her eyes, smiled encouragingly back and suggested that as she hadn't had a chance to finish her drink at the dance, perhaps she might care for one now.

'Yes,' said Belinda with relief. 'Yes please, I think I would.'

She sank down in a corner of one of the soft leather couches while Hal disappeared into the kitchen to make promising clinking noises with ice and glasses. In a moment he was back with two fluted goblets containing something bubbly, amber-coloured and inviting.

He lowered himself down beside her and raised his glass. 'To Belinda—who will never wear grey again.'

'To Hal—who will henceforth stop trying to dictate my life.'

Hal laughed softly. 'Don't be too sure of that, love.' He touched his glass to hers. 'My employees all tell me I was born to be a dictator.'

Belinda was just opening her mouth to tell him that she was not one of his employees, when their hands inadvertently touched and for a moment both of them were aware of a shattering shock. Their eyes met and locked in a hold of such electrifying intensity that if the house had fallen around their heads, neither of them would have been able to look away.

Without a word Hal put down his glass, leaned towards her, and took her drink from hand. Then he put both hands on her waist and drew her against his chest.

For a while they remained still, savouring the closeness and the warmth of each other's bodies. Then slowly, determinedly, Hal's lips came down over hers.

This time the wonder of his kiss was not new and unexpected, but more like a coming home, a return to a place known and greatly loved, yet which became more desirable and fascinating with each enchanting visit.

His lips explored and tasted every corner of her mouth as their tongues touched, and Belinda's arms went around his neck to push beneath his jacket. Her fingers kneaded the broadness of his back.

'Belinda,' groaned Hal, as he finally tore his mouth from hers and buried his face in her neck. 'Dear heaven, Belinda, you're so—so . . .' He stopped suddenly as he heard her draw in her breath. When he straightened he saw her flushed face staring up at him with an expression of almost childlike disappointment.

'What is it?' he asked. 'What have I done?'

'Nothing,' said Belinda, almost to herself, as a

dreamy, sensuous smile spread slowly across her face. 'Except that you've stopped kissing me.'

'Oh, dear heaven,' he said again. He stared into the luminous dark eyes which were turned so lovingly up to his. So *trustingly* up to his. And he remembered that this sweet, quiet, almost beautiful woman had never before been touched by any man. She could not possibly have any idea what she was doing—and to his bitter regret it was up to him to show her.

'Belinda,' he said roughly, 'I shouldn't have brought you here. I promised to take you dancing, and I didn't even let you finish one dance . . .'

'I don't mind that. I'd rather be here with you.'

He ignored her, searching for words she would understand. 'And you were right when you told me I behaved badly. Mrs Barclay will forgive me soon enough, but she's not likely to forgive you.'

How right he was, thought Belinda. His arrogant assumption that he could do whatever he pleased and get away with it was deplorably justified. She wondered if there was a woman on earth who could resist this man's magnetism for long. *She* couldn't any more. Nor did she want to.

Gently she put her hand up to smooth the grooves from between his eyes. 'I don't care about Mrs Barclay,' she said quietly. 'I only care about you.'

Hal muttered something unprintable under his breath, and pulled her hand forcefully from his face. 'Belinda, listen to me. I'm sorry. I must have been crazy back there in the dance hall. Drugged by the music and your eyes. But I was only thinking of myself. Because I want you—more than I've ever wanted a woman in my life . . .'

Belinda gazed steadily at the strong, ravaged face with damp glistening on his brow, his thick dark hair in disarray. She let her eyes stray down over his lean body with the shirt strained tight across his chest and his long legs stretched in front of him. And she knew that she wanted him too, more than she had ever wanted anyone—or anything—in her life.

Yes, she wanted him. And whatever she might decide in the future, tonight she was going to have him. She *would* have her night to remember. Fleetingly, her mind flew back over all the years when it had never occurred to her that she would ever need any man as she now so desperately needed Hal—who had suddenly and devastatingly adopted the role of gentleman.

Well, she could easily do something about that.

His hand was still on her wrist, and with her eyes smiling provocatively into his, she drew it towards her until his fist rested in the V of her low-cut gown.

He stared at her, his eyes dark with desire. 'Do you know what you're doing to me, woman?' he rasped.

'Yes. I do. Love me, Hal.'

Hal swore, a harsh grating sound that made her flinch, and then, as she put her free hand on his neck to tug at his tie, he suddenly seized both her wrists and held her away from him so that she was pressed against the black leather arm of the couch.

For a moment his tormented gaze pinned her in a hold that was so physical she could feel it, then his features seemed to darken as he said in a hard, callous voice which she didn't recognise, 'All right, Belinda. I tried. Lord knows I tried. But I'm not a saint. I'm a man, and I have a man's needs . . .'

'I have needs too, Hal. Love me. Please.'

With a wrenching groan Hal released her wrists, and the next instant he was leaning over her, his fingers in the soft curls of her hair. Belinda put her hands up to his face to pull it down to hers as their lips met in a long, almost savage kiss. For just a flash of time, she was frightened by the ardour of his passion, but then her own hunger, for so many years unacknowledged, rose in her like an ember which rapidly created an inferno as she cried out, 'Hal! Please . . .'

He sat up then, his breathing ragged. 'Belinda, are you sure?'

She could see the extraordinary effort it cost him to stay in control, and all of a sudden she knew the meaning of the words 'banked fires'. And the banks were going to break at any moment, for both of them.

'Yes,' she said, knowing that she had never been so certain of anything in her life. 'Yes, Hal. I'm sure.'

With a muffled exclamation he pushed himself to his feet, bent over her and picked her up in his arms. As she buried her face against his shoulder she could feel his heart thundering in his chest.

In two strides he was across the floor. Then he was carrying her down a short hallway and kicking open the white-painted door of his bedroom. Belinda clung tightly to his neck, but almost at once she felt her hands being summarily unclasped as she was deposited with scant ceremony on the bed.

She opened her eyes. The light was on and she was vaguely conscious of black sheets. And after that all she saw was Hal, who was staring down at her, a magnificent male animal with the strength of his desire for her evident in every taut line of his body.

She held out her arms, and with another groan he was lying beside her, his hands on the fastening at the back of her dress. Then the dress was at the foot of the bed and Hal was removing the wisps of blue lace which were all that remained between her body and his eyes.

She had bought those wisps at the last moment without ever admitting to herself the hope that had been at the back of her mind.

Somehow his tie and jacket had already found their way to the floor, tentatively, she reached out her hands to release the buttons of his shirt.

'Belinda.' His mouth found her breasts. 'Oh, Belinda.'

Her fingers tangled in the thickness of his hair as she let out an unconscious little cry.

Now there was no barrier between them, only the softness of her body moving against the hardness of his, and somehow she knew that Hal was controlling his need for her with an enormous effort of will as his hands moved tantalisingly down her sides, feathered over thighs and abdomen, explored the smooth roundness of her bottom . . .

Her body was on fire, consumed with the desire to be part of him, consumed with a desperate hunger that she had waited all her life to appease. She ran her hands over his chest, up over his shoulders, digging her fingers into the muscles across his back. Hal's lips covered hers then and, very gently, he parted her thighs.

For all their passionate hunger, in the end their coming together was slow and incredibly tender, as Hal took infinite care, because it was the first time for Belinda, that it should be just as wonderful for her as it was for him.

And it was. For one moment there was pain—and then it was gone, flowing upwards into the joy and completion of being one with Hal. Because she loved Hal. She knew that now, beyond any shadow of doubt.

There were other shadows, but as she lay in his arms, lost in the darkness of his eyes which were smiling into hers with a deep and tender warmth, she was not aware of shadows. Only of the release and happiness of the moment.

'My lovely Belinda.' Hal smoothed the dark curls gently back from her forehead. 'Do you know that you've given me the most wonderful gift in the world?'

'No,' said Belinda. 'No Hal. The giving was all yours.'

He shook his head. 'Ours, love. We gave to each other. At least . . .' He lifted himself on one elbow and gazed down at her, his face suddenly registering concern. 'I didn't hurt you, did I? I tried not to.'

'No.' She smiled at him, a soft, seductive smile. 'I don't think you could ever hurt me, Hal.'

For a second his eyes clouded, became distant and mysteriously opaque. 'Don't say that, Belinda.'

'Why not?' She ran a hand across the black hair on his chest.

'Because—another woman said it to me once. A very long time ago.'

She felt a sharp jab of fear. 'And did you hurt her?'

'Perhaps not.' He smiled, a little too quickly. 'Let's forget it.'

She nodded, but her eyes clouded now, because his reference to the past had made her remember the future. With difficulty, she smiled back at him. 'All right, we'll forget it,' she agreed quietly.

There could be no future tonight. Only the present. Only Hal, who would be hers for a few hours longer.

For a while they lay together, her head on his shoulder, and both of them at peace. Then after a time his thumb stroked softly down her cheek and he turned to look at her, eyes shining with a tender sensuality. And Belinda's hand moved to his waist, tracing over his skin as she began to explore the body of this man she was just beginning to know.

'Witch,' he murmured, cupping her breasts and turning to cover every inch of her body with kisses.

Soon they made love again, and Belinda, to whom love was such an unexpected miracle, was amazed to discover that the second time was just as wonderful as the first.

Hours later she looked at the big gold clock on the wall and saw that it was almost morning.

'I have to go,' she exclaimed. 'Jack Oliphant. He'll wonder where on earth I am.'

Hal grinned, and stretched his arms lazily above his head. 'Jack Oliphant won't wonder at all. He'll know exactly where you are.'

'That's even more reason to get back,' groaned Belinda.

Hal's grin broadened into a leer. 'I told you I'd ruin you reputation.'

Belinda gave an exasperated sigh and threw her legs determinedly over the side of the bed. 'Yes, but I didn't think you meant it literally. Hal, I promised Jack I'd be home by two. And it's *morning*.'

'Not quite. But I suppose if you insist . . .'

'I do.'

He shrugged and lay back against the pillows looking maddeningly indolent and unruffled as he watched her scramble into the royal blue dress.

'It's back to front,' he remarked blandly, after she had carefully pulled it down over her head.

'You might have told me,' she complained, pulling it off again and giving him what she hoped was a quelling glare.

'I might have. But I didn't.' He stretched again and settled the sheet comfortably below his waist.

Belinda paused in her struggle to fasten the dress. 'Why black sheets, Hal?' she asked suspiciously. It had suddenly occurred to her that black sheets held a strong connotation of pre-planning—or else a complacent assurance that he need never sleep alone unless he chose to.

Hal raised a mocking eyebrow. 'Why not?'

'Because—because . . .'

'Because they're altogether too sinful?' His irresistible lips were parting in a white-toothed grin that would have made Belinda want to kick him if he hadn't suddenly reached out his arms and pulled her down on top of him on the bed.

'Yes,' she said, giving up and laughing into his face. 'Much too sinful.'

'All right.' He sighed with feigned resignation and ran a finger lightly down her spine. 'All right. Just for you I'll replace them with suitably chaste pink ones. With flowers. Do you think you'd fancy me on pink flowers?'

'No,' said Belinda with feeling. 'I'm sure I shouldn't fancy you at all.'

'Good. I'm relieved. In that case I shall stick to basic black.'

'Yes, you'd better. And you'd also better get up. I need a ride back home.'

'No, you don't. Stay and have breakfast with me.'

'Hal, I warn you . . .' began Belinda.

'What do you warn me?'

'If you don't get up right now and drive me home, I'll—I'll . . .'

'Phone up Mrs Barclay and ask her to give you a lift?' he suggested wickedly.

'Hal! Don't even think of it. Please get up.'

Reluctantly, and with a very bad grace, Hal did as he

was asked, and fifteen minutes later the Mercedes was purring through the pink-tinged streets as the sun came up over the horizon.

'I'll see you tomorrow. After the shop closes,' said Hal as he pulled up at her door. 'Be good. And Belinda—thank you.' He dropped a quick kiss on her nose, and before Belinda could think of a reply he had vanished down the lane into the dawn.

It *is* tomorrow, thought Belinda, as she pushed the door open on the sleepy figure of Jack, who pushed himself hastily to his feet and equally hastily smothered a knowing grin.

Yes, it was tomorrow. The future which she had put on hold for one evening was already beginning to unfold.

For the remainder of the morning Belinda wandered round in a daze. She fed the animals, heated a bran muffin which, when she bit into it, turned out to be three congealed figs, and told Joe when he called that yes, the dress had been right on—while trying not to betray that it had actually been right off.

When she caught herself putting a roast in the oven still nicely wrapped in plastic and styrofoam, she decided that perhaps she ought to get some sleep.

She pulled on her plain cotton nightgown, lay down on the bed and closed her eyes. But sleep didn't come. Instead, a vision of Hal's rugged features floated behind her eyelids and her body rekindled with his remembered warmth. Her mind began to go round in circles.

She had wanted last night to happen and had thought that one night would be enough. Now she knew it wasn't because she could never have enough of Hal.

What should she do? What *could* she do? He had said he would see her this evening, but what of the future?

When she had asked him if he was planning to move away soon he had certainly not denied it. In fact the question had seemed to annoy him. Anyway what did she want to happen? The truth was she didn't know herself. For now, she supposed all she could hope for was that things would go on as they were—and that soon last night would be repeated . . .

Last night . . . a smile spread softly over her face. All these years, and she hadn't known . . . But then perhaps she had been waiting for Hal . . .

Gradually her body relaxed, and in a few minutes she was sound asleep.

After what seemed like no time at all, but was in fact almost two hours, she was abruptly awakened by the piercing sound of her doorbell. Mentally making a note to rip the thing out of the wall and replace it with coyly insipid chimes she could ignore, Belinda pulled on her robe and staggered out to open the door.

'Delivery for you,' announced the man who stood on the doorstep. He gestured at a large van which was pulled up at the entrance to the lane.

'Oh. Yes. Thank you.' Belinda remembered Hal's promise to send her a new bicycle and prepared to see it lifted to the ground.

But it wasn't a bicycle the man retrieved from the front seat of his van, but a small package in a paper bag stamped 'Cinnamon Jewellers'. Mystified, she thanked him again and carried it into the cottage.

Inside the bag was a small white leather box with a card attached to it. But all the card said was, 'I changed my mind. Love, Hal.'

Frowning, she opened the lid. And then she gasped.

On a black velvet cushion lay a circlet of shimmering—diamonds? Yes, they had to be diamonds.

Slowly she picked up the delicate bangle and, even more slowly, slipped it over her wrist.

A diamond bracelet. Not a bicycle. What was it Hal had said? That jewellery was often offered in expectation of—services in return?

A dull flush crept up over her pale cheeks and she let out a short, incoherent cry. Misty, lying in a sunbeam by the window, lifted her ears and ambled over to see what was the matter. But Belinda was staring down at the bracelet as if it were a scorpion about to bite her, and as she tore it off her wrist and threw it away from her on to the table, she didn't even notice the little dog sitting worriedly at her feet.

Service in return. Was that what she had done for him last night? Performed a service? For which he was now offering payment? When he had left, his last words had been 'thank you'. Thank you for relieving an itch? Was that all it had been to him? She remembered the black sheets—and the lack of willing women in Cinnamon Bay.

Belinda groped behind her, could not immediately lay her hands on a chair and, in desperation, sank down on to the floor. Hopelessly she wrapped her arms around her ankles and let her forehead droop against her knees.

For a long time she sat there, feeling but not thinking, and then, dazedly, she lifted her eyes. What had she expected, anyway? Hal had never said he loved her. She wasn't even sure that was what she wanted, because although she had no doubt she loved *him*, she was also certain her father had been right when he said that love was a risky business. And as long as Hal didn't love her, it was a risk she wouldn't have to take. At least—it had seemed that way at one time . . .

All right, so he didn't love her. That was fair enough.

But this gift, it made her feel soiled somehow, like some sleazy commodity he had to pay for, not really a woman . . .

Suddenly she felt dirty. She had had a bath when she came in, but now she needed to wash all over again. Without being aware of it, she gave a little moan, jumped up from the floor and stumbled across the hall to the bathroom.

A few minutes later she was lying in hot, soapy water scrubbing at her pink skin as if her life depended on getting it clean.

At exactly six o'clock that evening Belinda stood at the sink peeling potatoes to go with the roast—now minus plastic—that she was cooking in case Hal chose to stay for supper.

In the interval between the delivery of the bracelet and the time she had to start cooking, she had come to the conclusion that there was nothing whatever to be gained by refusing to see him. In fact she wanted to see him so that she could tell him, at considerable length, exactly how she felt about his gift. It was the only way she could think of to salvage what was left of her pride, and if this meant she had to feed him, then so be it. She didn't even acknowledge the faint hope in some corner of her mind that her interpretation of his gift might be mistaken.

She was gazing grimly at the wall, deciding that Hal was bound to be the sort of man who wouldn't eat broccoli, when a loud knock sounded on the door and she almost stabbed the peeler into her arm.

Belinda sighed. She couldn't win. The doorbell invariably shattered her eardrums, but when people knocked it wasn't any better. The world seemed possessed by an irresistible urge to destroy her peace. No, she amended, as the knocking ceased and turned into a man's voice shouting. Not the world. Just Hal.

She put down the peeler, crossed the room unhurriedly and, as the noise from outside increased in volume, slowly opened the door.

Hal stood on the step wearing well-pressed brown slacks and a tweed jacket. One of his arms was raised to knock again. The other held a huge bunch of flowers—irises, in a deep and luminous blue.

'There's no necessity to behave like a gorilla on the rampage,' said Belinda frostily.

Hal's mouth, which had broken into a grin when she appeared, clamped tightly shut again, and he fixed her with a keen, discerning stare. Then under his breath he murmured something which sounded like, 'The return of the porcupine.' His next words were unmistakable. 'I don't believe I'm a gorilla, love, but if you don't let me in this minute I may very well go on the rampage.'

Silently Belinda stepped back to allow him to pass.

'Well,' he said, as usual filling the kitchen with his presence, 'I'm glad to see you've taken my advice about locking doors.'

'Not consciously. It just happened to be locked. And there was no need to start shouting like a . . .'

'Yes, there was. I'm not a patient man, Belinda.'

'So I've noticed.' She turned away from him and made her way back to the sink.

The next moment she felt his hand grip her arm as he swung her back to face him. 'What's this? Why the cold shoulder?' His voice and his eyes, which she knew could be so loving, were suddenly hard as stone. And the flowers he held were brushing against her face. 'Here. Take them.' He thrust them at her, and she had no choice but to do as he said before they dropped on the floor. 'I chose them because blue is so obviously your colour,' he told her. The words were sheer flattery, but there was nothing remotely flattering about his reserved and distant voice.

'Thank you.' Her voice was equally reserved and distant as she took a vase from the cupboard and began to arrange the irises in water.

Hal leaned against the wall with his arms crossed, watching her from under half-closed lids. 'All right,' he said, the moment she had finished. 'Now what's this all about, Belinda? I thought we'd got past the cat-and-mouse stage. So cut it out. Because I've had just about enough of this game.'

'Oh!' spluttered Belinda, wiping her hands agitatedly up and down her jeans. 'Oh! How dare you? How *could* you?'

'How could I what?' Hal's jaw jutted belligerently and his fists were bunched tightly on his thighs.

Belinda was conscious as she had never been before of the power behind his vibrant masculinity. For one moment she was afraid of him, and then the force of her own pain and hurt took over, as she shouted, 'How *could* you treat me like—like one of your—your paid *women*?' She put a wealth of contempt in the word. 'You know. The kind you bribe with diamonds.' She raised her arm to brush away a tear which was inexplicably swimming down her cheek. 'You're a jerk, Hal Blake. A callous, arrogant, unfeeling, self-satisfied jerk. That's what you are.'

'Have you finished?' Hal's voice was hard and controlled. So was his body, which she could see was held rigidly in check.

'No. I haven't finished.'

'Oh, yes, you have.' In one stride Hal was across the kitchen and she found herself jolted against his chest. 'Now you start making sense, young lady, or it won't be diamonds I'll be giving you. And that's a promise.'

'Just because you're bigger than I am . . .'

'No, *not* just because I'm bigger. Because, as I told you, I'm not a patient man and you're trying me very hard.'

Belinda stared up into his face, dark with anger and with an odd little pulse she had never noticed before beating at the side of his neck. And then she saw his eyes, deep-set and furious—and there was something behind them, something that was more pain than anger. Something that was—simple confusion?

She took a long, deep breath, all at once unbearably aware of his nearness. 'Why?' she asked steadily. 'Why, Hal?'

'Why are you trying my patience?' He sounded incredulous.

'No. Why did you give me the bracelet?'

'What?' A dozen conflicting emotions crossed his face, and as Belinda watched, unable to look away, she saw anger change to confusion then indignation and, finally, if she was reading him right, to the beginnings of understanding.

'Oh, no!' he exclaimed, releasing her so abruptly she nearly fell into the sink. 'Do you mean to tell me . . .? No, you *couldn't* think that.' He closed his eyes. When he opened them again he looked straight into hers and said disbelievingly, 'You don't think I gave you that bracelet as payment for . . .' He pulled a face, and suddenly she saw the glimmerings of a smile. 'For—services rendered?'

Belinda frowned, feeling ridiculously naïve and

foolish. If he hadn't given her the bracelet for that, then . . . 'I don't understand,' she said quickly. 'You said last night that you give jewellery to women for—for that reason.'

'No, I didn't. Although in the past . . .' His eyes gleamed with a brief reminiscence and he touched his hand to his mouth. 'Never mind. What I said was that gifts of that sort can sometimes be construed that way.'

'Exactly. So you see . . .'

'No, I don't see, Belinda. That's not why I gave *you* diamonds.'

'Oh.' She gazed at him doubtfully, her eyes so big that Hal wanted desperately to take her into his arms.

But instead he said softly, not daring to set her off again by rushing things, 'I gave you that bracelet because I care for you, Belinda. Because you're my beautiful, funny, prickly little porcupine. Don't you understand? You've given me so much that I wanted to give you something special in return.' His lips twisted. 'But my mother is right. I'm an insensitive clod at times. I should have known . . .'

Oh, lord. She *had* been wrong about him. How could she have been such a fool?

'No,' she cried. 'No, you're not, Hal. I was the clod, not you and I'm so very sorry.' She looked down at the tiled floor. 'But still—I can't—I shouldn't . . .'

'Shouldn't what?'

'I can't possibly accept your gift.'

'Why not?'

'Because it's too—too . . .'

'Compromising?' His long lashes covered his eyes so that she couldn't see his expression, but she knew his anger was gone, because he was laughing at her. With good reason.

'It's too late for that, isn't it?' she said with overplayed resignation.

Hal looked up swiftly, and saw that she was laughing too.

'Much too late,' he said roughly, and took her into his arms.

'So you'll keep the bracelet?' he whispered, when their differences had been settled, in time-honoured fashion, with a kiss.

'I—yes. Thank you, Hal. It's beautiful.'

Much later, after a passionate interlude on the living-room sofa which Misty took a very dim view of, Hal remarked that whatever she had in the oven smelled as if it was reaching a stage of advanced cremation.

'Oh, lord,' Belinda cried, leaping up and falling over an increasingly indignant Misty. 'That's your supper.'

'Mm.' Hal wrinkled his nose and wandered into the kitchen behind her with his jacket swung carelessly across his shoulder. 'Cremated pot roast and raw potatoes. Is this a sample of your culinary ability, my love?'

Belinda aimed a swipe at him with her oven cloth, and went on rescuing the roast.

'Because if it is,' he continued imperturbably, 'I think I shall have to reconsider my intentions.'

'What intentions?' asked Belinda abstractedly, pushing the remains of the roast on to a wooden cutting-board and flinging the half-peeled potatoes frantically into a pot.

'Well,' drawled Hal, putting his hands in his pockets and contemplating the ceiling, 'I *was* going to ask you to marry me, but under the circumstances . . .' He nodded at Belinda's burnt offering. 'Under the circumstances, I'm not sure my digestion would stand it.'

CHAPTER EIGHT

BELINDA heard him while she was busy prodding the meat to see if any of it was edible. But the words were spoken lightly—not as if he meant them—and when it came right down to it, she didn't want to believe what he was saying. Any talk of marriage made her wary, and, although she loved Hal, she didn't think he loved her. Wanted her, yes. Liked her, and enjoyed her company. But loved? No. It wasn't likely, was it?

And even supposing he does love you, a small voice whispered in her ear, you know what happens to love the moment the wedding bells stop ringing.

She glanced doubtfully up at him, saw that his eyes were fixed on her with a teasing, expectant glint, and without answering, busied herself with the broccoli.

'Well?' said Hal. He directed a questioning eyebrow at the back of her curly head. 'Aren't you going to say something? I don't like broccoli, by the way.'

'I didn't think you would,' replied Belinda, continuing to chop it into sections.

Hal's eyes narrowed, and without a word he reached over her shoulder, removed the knife from her hand and, taking hold of both her elbows, pulled her firmly away from the sink. Then he wrapped his arms securely under her breasts and held her against him so that she couldn't move.

'Answer me,' he ordered, with his chin resting on her hair.

'What do you mean?' Once again his closeness was playing incredible havoc with her heartbeat, and she could feel all the lithe male length of him against her back.

'Belinda,' he said, a touch of velvet steel in his voice, 'I asked you to marry me. And I don't find your absorption with broccoli a particularly flattering response.'

'Oh.'

'Well?' Velvet steel now strongly laced with impatience.

Oh, dear. She wasn't going to be able to evade him any longer, or pretend that she didn't understand. Unless . . .

'You didn't actually ask me to marry you,' she pointed out, on a curious, breathless gasp. 'Actually you said your digestion wouldn't stand it.'

'Belinda, don't prevaricate.' Gently he removed his arms from around her ribs. 'Look at me.'

She didn't want to look at him, she wanted to chop broccoli. But she couldn't ignore the authority in his voice. Reluctantly she turned around and raised her eyes to somewhere near the level of his jaw.

'I said look at me.'

Again the tone of command that she couldn't ignore. Very slowly she lifted her head until she was looking directly into his eyes.

'That's better. Belinda, love, I know I'm not always good at expressing my feelings. But I do promise you I'm not just looking for a cook. If I were, you'd fill the bill admirably, as I have very good reason to know.' He smiled, and his smile was so soft and sensual that Belinda could barely prevent herself from reaching up to put her arms round his neck. 'I love you, Belinda Porcupine. Goodness knows I didn't mean to. I thought my foot-loose life suited me down to the ground—until

I went away to Vancouver and discovered that I missed you like hell and just couldn't wait to get back to you. Then last night . . .' He paused and took her hands in his. 'Belinda, I'm asking you again, properly this time. Will you marry me?'

Dear lord, he did love her. At least he said he did, although she still had trouble believing it.

But it was no good. It wouldn't work

She shook her head wordlessly, then opened her mouth to answer and found that she couldn't speak. Finally, with enormous effort, she managed to croak in a hoarse, ugly voice which she hardly recognised as her own, 'No. No, Hal. I can't.'

He stared at her, his eyebrows jutting darkly over eyes she couldn't bear to look at. 'Why not? I know you're not indifferent to me. I can give you anything you want, take you away from all this . . .' He waved a disparaging arm around the kitchen. 'You wouldn't even have to cook unless you wanted to. And you and Jerry get along like bread and jam . . .'

'Yes, yes I know. I love Jerry,' she interrupted. 'I—I love *you*, Hal. But I don't want to be taken away from all this . . .'

'Then we'll stay in Cinnamon Bay. I can run the business from here.'

'Yes, but . . .' Her voice rose on a note of desperation. 'Hal, I don't *want* to marry you. I don't want to marry anyone.'

There was something in his eyes now that went beyond pain or wounded pride. Was it anguish? No, she decided. It was anger. Anger and, after a long silence, contempt.

'You're afraid to, aren't you?' he said bitterly. 'Afraid to trust, afraid to give yourself. You'd rather hide behind ugly grey clothes and some flimsy excuse from the past—your father perhaps, or that spotty youth who didn't want to take you to the dance. You don't even know how to love, do you, Belinda?' Suddenly his hand was gripping her shoulder. 'You'll regret it one day, you know, when you find out life has passed you by and you're nothing but a lonely, embittered old woman living by yourself in the backwoods—with other people's pets.'

Belinda understood that his own disappointment and hurt were at the back of this cruel cascade of hostile words. But the knowledge didn't lessen her own hurt. She lowered her eyes, fixed them on the sensual lips which had become so brutally hard—and gradually she became conscious that the pain was not only in her heart. It was, quite literally, in her shoulder, because his thumb was digging so deeply into her skin that it hurt her.

'Please, you're hurting me,' she whispered.

Hal stared at the hand that was holding her as if he had no idea how it had got there. Immediately he released her as if she were too hot to touch. 'I'm sorry, I didn't realise . . .' When he saw the bewilderment and misery in her eyes he added harshly, 'I *am* sorry, Belinda. I wanted to marry you, not to make you cry.'

'I'm not crying.'

It wasn't true. She could hardly see him any more through the mist in front of her eyes.

'Yes, you are.' Very gently now he pulled her into his arms and held her. 'I didn't mean those things, Belinda. I lost my temper.'

'I know you did,' she murmured, hiding her face against his shirt so that he couldn't see her tears. 'It's all right. I'm sorry too.'

And she was sorry. Sorry she had hurt him, sorry that she couldn't marry him, and especially sorry that, although he said he hadn't meant it, Hal thought she lacked the courage to take a risk.

Was he right? Maybe. She didn't think so though. Marriages that seemed to be made in heaven were always turning into hell. Her parents' union had ended in grief and heartbreak, as had Anthea's two devastating mistakes. Oh, yes, her resistance to orange blossom and church bells was rooted in clear-headed common sense. Of that she was completely convinced.

Hal was still holding her, and if he was bleeding inside he didn't show it.

'Come on,' he said encouragingly. 'If we must have that horrible green stuff, let's get the show on the road.'

She nodded without speaking, and with Hal's help the broccoli and potatoes were soon on plates on the table. When he tried to slice the meat for her, though, it proved a task beyond even his considerable strength.

'You've just invented Canada's ultimate weapon,' he remarked drily. 'You're about to make a fortune, my dear.'

Belinda laughed shakily, and fifteen minutes later they sat down to a meal of reheated broccoli, potatoes—and scrambled eggs.

When the silence between them became uncomfortable, Belinda jumped up to put on a record, which gave Hal the opportunity to make remarks about what he called her infernally loud taste in music. Relieved to be back on a familiar and safe bone of contention, she retaliated with her own candid comments on his lack of musical taste. The rest of the meal passed relatively smoothly to the accompaniment of superficial, slightly forced, banter about noise.

Belinda noticed that Hal also concentrated a lot of his attention on a devoted Misty, whose attitude of worshipful adoration changed to injured disgust when he tried to feed her his broccoli.

When they had finished Hal helped her to clear away the dishes, and shortly after that he said it was time for him to leave.

Belinda saw him to the door. It was a warm night and his jacket and tie were slung over one shoulder again as he said goodnight. She stared at the enticing V of the white shirt open just below his throat.

Briefly he looked down at her, but the expression on his face now was withdrawn and enigmatic. 'I'll see you tomorrow, Belinda. Think about what I said.' He bent down, ran a hand surprisingly over her bottom, and kissed her very lightly on the cheek.

Then he was gone.

'Yes,' Belinda murmured after him. 'I'll think about it.'

But she knew she wouldn't.

As it turned out, in a sense Belinda did consider Hal's proposal. Not with any idea of accepting, but because, however hard she tried to, she couldn't keep her mind off the scene of the night before.

The trouble was that every time she started to do anything, even if it was only a matter of refilling the dogs' water bowl or cleaning out a cage, Hal's face seemed to intrude—and, instead of concentrating on the task in hand, she would discover herself staring blankly at an empty bowl or putting a disgruntled mouse back in a dirty cage.

When, in the late afternoon of the day following Hal's unexpected declaration, she realised that she had forgotten to take Misty for her morning walk, forgotten to eat either lunch or breakfast, and only just remembered in time that she had already fed three dogs and a very fat cat, none of whom needed an extra meal, she came to the conclusion that this nonsense could not go on. Her obsession with Hal Blake must be taken in hand, weighed, and put neatly away in some compartment of her mind without a key.

Right, she decided, giving a quick pat to one of the dogs and closing the door to his run. First things first. Are you going to marry Hal, Belinda? No. She was not. That was not on the cards. Fine. So what *are* you going to do then? Nothing. Great. And how long do you expect him to stick around now that he's got the marriage bug into his head? He probably wants a mother for Jerry.

Yes, she agreed with herself. He probably does, because in spite of all his denials he does feel guilty about not providing a stable home for his son.

Belinda sank down in the blue print chair that matched the sofa and stared gloomily at a fly which was buzzing on the sunlit window. Hal said he loved her. So why couldn't things just go on as they were? They may for a while, that annoying voice pointed out, but sooner or later he'll give up and go away.

He will anyway, Belinda argued. A marriage certificate didn't stop my father from leaving my mother. In fact he always said that 'damned piece of paper' was what actually made him leave.

She ran a hand wearily through her hair. All right, so what alternative was there? Absolutely none. She would just have to take each day as it came.

Belinda was still hunched in the chair looking vulnerable and dejected when Hal arrived an hour later wearing shorts and an unbuttoned brown shirt which proved that it wasn't just his face that sported a tan.

'You left your door unlocked again,' he said censoriously. What he really wanted to do was take the drooping figure in his arms.

'Did I? Why are you wearing a towel around your neck?'

'Because we're going swimming. And don't change the subject. You'll get yourself raped one of these days, Belinda.' She really did scare him with her casual disregard for elementary safety precautions.

'Will I?' she replied without much interest. 'That'll be a nice change.' Belinda had been brooding all day and she was in no mood to listen to Hal's strictures about locks.

'Damn it, woman,' he shouted, flaring up out of all proportion. 'Haven't you got any sense in that black curly head of yours? You're behaving like a dim-witted little idiot who's asking for all the trouble she can get.'

Hal hadn't had a good day either.

'I'm not asking for anything. And do stop shouting, Hal.'

'I wouldn't need to shout if you weren't such a . . .'

'I know. Dim-witted little idiot. Hal, if you just came over to yell at me, why don't you—go and—and have your swim?'

'I didn't just come over to . . .' He took a deep breath and forced his voice down an octave. 'I didn't just come over to yell at you. I came to take you swimming. I've spoken to Joe. He'll be over in a minute.'

'A bit high-handed of you, wasn't it? How do you know I even want to go?'

'I don't,' said Hal through gritted teeth, 'but I do know *I* want to throw you into the sea—with the pleasurable option of drowning you if it'll make you see some kind of sense.'

'I don't think I'd see anything much if I were drowned,' remarked Belinda woodenly. Then, realising the conversation was getting out of hand, her wide mouth parted in a slightly weary smile. 'Look, if it will make you feel any better, I will try to remember to lock the door.'

Hal crossed the room and sat on the arm of her chair. 'It would make me feel a whole lot better, Belinda. I don't want anyone raping you but me.'

This promising beginning was interrupted by the arrival of Joe, who had also walked through the open door, and looked excessively smug when he saw Hal and Belinda intimately entwined in the chair.

Belinda gave him an embarrassed glare which forbade him to make any comment, and hurried off to her room to get changed.

'I don't have a bathing-suit,' she told Hal, as the Blake Bicycles truck jolted them on to the beach. She assumed that the Mercedes was altogether too aristocratic for such a plebeian pastime as swimming.

Hal raised his eyebrows. 'I can hardly wait.'

'So I'm wearing my shorts and a tank-top,' she finished hastily.

'Ah. Such disappointing propriety.'

Belinda laughed for the first time that day, and didn't tell him that his own bronzed, tough body in very brief white trunks stopped only just short of being immoral by merely existing.

The next moment Hal had seized her hand and was towing her into the water. It was a calm, still evening and the sun glowed with a burning orange flame on the horizon. But it was still only May, and as Belinda's toes hit the water she gasped.

'It's cold,' she wailed.

Hal paid no attention and dragged her in up to her waist.

'I'm not going in,' cried Belinda, pulling back.

'Sure you are.' Laughing, Hal grabbed her around the waist and dunked her in up to her neck.

'Aah-h. You fiend. You meant it, didn't you? But you're not going to drown me, Hal, you're going to freeze me to death.' Belinda shivered.

'Cold, love? I'll warm you.' Suddenly all solicitous concern, Hal lifted her out of the water and held her against his bare, wet chest.

She could feel all his muscled strength, all his desire, through the thin, saturated fabric of her clothes—and in spite of herself she did feel warmer, especially when Hal bent his head to taste her salt-brushed mouth.

It was a long, salty and very passionate kiss, and when it was over Hal, breathing hard, suggested that they should be getting home.

He meant his home, and, as on the previous occasion when she had been there, their soaked clothing was soon piled on the floor while, locked in each other's arms, they tumbled on to Hal's cool and sinful black sheets.

Again it was wonderful, almost as it had been the first time. And yet—somehow there was something which was not the same. Not an inhibition exactly, because they loved each other with the same violent hunger as before, but a sense of wariness, of something held back—and Belinda knew that it was because she had not been able to accept all of Hal, and that, because she would make no permanent commitment to him, he would never again give all of himself to her.

She knew a great sense of loss. But most of Hal was still better than none of him, and she would settle for whatever she could have, for just as long as she could have it.

As it happened, she had it for exactly one week.

Hal continued to arrive at Belinda's door, now locked to avoid further controversy, every evening after the bike shop closed. They swam, made love, went dancing in Nanaimo once, made love again, had two candlelit dinners at the Inn—and they talked, although never about the subject that was uppermost in both their minds.

By the end of the week Hal knew all there was to know about Belinda's solitary but not altogether unhappy childhood, and she knew all about his upbringing as the only child of two very opinionated, reasonably well-off parents who often left him in the care of Hattie, the family's devoted but over-indulgent housekeeper. Hal said his parents had only themselves to blame for the fact that he had chosen to go into bicycles instead of law as they wanted, because in order to survive in that dogmatic household it had been essential for him to be even more stubborn and contrary than they were.

'Otherwise I'd have been reduced to very flat squashed jelly,' he told her, grinning wryly.

Belinda had difficulty imagining anyone less likely to be reduced to squashed jelly than Hal, but she didn't say so because she was wondering why, in all this plethora of reminiscences, he had never once mentioned his wife. She knew his marriage hadn't worked, but had there been *no* good moments to remember?

The day before the end, they were lying, sated, but still with that indefinable barrier between them, on the pillows of Hal's large and comfortable bed. Afterwards

Belinda remembered every detail of the high white ceiling, from the grainy area in one corner where the painter had not quite done his job, to the mark above the window where Hal said he had once thrown a glass of wine in a fit of irritation at a fly.

She was staring at the clear, crystal globe of the light when Hal said, very quietly for him, 'I'll be leaving Cinnamon Bay soon, Belinda. It's time for me to move on. Have you thought about what I asked you?'

'Yes—no,' she whispered, as black panic began to rise up from her toes.

Hal turned his head away. He was still holding her against his shoulder, but now he sounded totally withdrawn and detached. 'I thought not. Think about it, then. Tomorrow I'll ask again.'

Soon afterwards she insisted he drive her home.

Tomorrow . . . she had until tomorrow to make up her mind forever.

Belinda lay in her own small bed and looked straight ahead into the darkness. Hal hadn't actually said it would be her last chance, but somehow it had been implicit in his words. And she *couldn't* accept him. She didn't *want* to marry him. She just wanted him to be with her, to continue to be part of her life.

'Damn you, Hal Blake,' she muttered into the empty room. 'I was happy before you came.'

Not ecstatically happy, she admitted grudgingly, but peaceful in her own contented way. She hadn't minded being alone, in fact she had liked it. And if she let him uproot her now from everything she had worked for she would be a thousand times more devastated when he left.

Because leave her he would in the end, she was utterly certain of that. That 'piece of paper' only made men feel restricted, and sooner or later they wanted to break the chain. After all, Hal's first marriage had ended in chaos, even if, apparently, that had not been entirely his fault.

Sleeplessly, Belinda tossed back and forth on the bed, and in the morning, when she got up and looked in the mirror, she decided her face would not make good propaganda for the beautifying effects of love.

'You look like the sort of dubious glob I sometimes find mouldering in the corner of my fridge,' remarked Hal when he arrived as promised that evening. 'Green around the edges and unappetising. What on earth have you been doing to yourself, Belinda?'

'You always were a great boost to my morale,' she replied morosely. 'If you really want to know, I couldn't sleep.'

'Neither could I.' Hal's eyes studied her dispassionately, and then he jerked his head at the living-room and suggested she had better sit down.

She nodded and made her way over to the flowered sofa, but instead of sitting beside her Hal lowered himself into the armchair opposite and crossed one ankle casually over his knee. Belinda, staring at his strong, square-tipped fingers resting lightly on the arms of the chair, felt something cold and unhappy stir in the pit of her stomach. Something that was a premonition of loss.

'Do you want me to take you out for dinner?' Hal asked surprisingly. 'Or shall I make you my speciality? Obviously you're not capable of cooking tonight.'

'Of course I am,' snapped Belinda. 'Just because I once overcooked the roast . . .'

'No, not because of that. Because you look ill.' He didn't smile at her, but his voice was full of puzzled concern. Belinda felt a tremor of relief. Perhaps he wouldn't force her to make irrevocable decisions after all. Not today.

'What's your speciality?' she asked, trying to sound brighter than she felt.

'Spaghetti. What else? Isn't that the ultimate stand-by of all the best lazy cooks?'

'I suppose so, but it's a very good stand-by.' She eyed him doubtfully. 'If you don't like cooking, why don't you get someone to do it for you?'

'I do sometimes. Mrs Oliphant's a very good cooker and cleaner when I ask her. But unfortunately, in the course of what my mother calls "all that unnecessary roaming", I have sometimes found myself without an immediate source of slave labour—that's my mother's charming way of putting it too—and, as I have a deep-rooted prejudice against starvation, I have on occasions found it necessary to produce my own meals. Besides, one large pot of spaghetti can last me for almost a week.'

'Hm.' Belinda wrinkled her nose. 'By that time it must look about as green and unappetising as I do.'

Hal smiled. 'I've changed my mind about you, though. You could never look truly unappetising. Are we going to risk my spaghetti?'

'All right. I think you'll find what you need in the kitchen.' She really was too tired—and too anxious—to think about food tonight.

An hour later she thought Misty must be playing tug-o-war with her shoulder. But when her eyes flew open she discovered, not Misty, but Hal, standing over her shaking her briskly.

'Wake up. You needn't think you'll escape my *haute cuisine* that easily.'

'Huh? What?' Belinda blinked at him owlishly. 'Oh. I guess I must have fallen asleep.'

'No guessing about it. Come on.' He took both her wrists, pulled her off the sofa and with his hand in the small of her back propelled her firmly into the kitchen.

The spaghetti was a surprisingly tasty concoction for someone who said he didn't like to cook, and by the time they had finished eating, Belinda was beginning to feel that she might be ready to rejoin the human race—provided Hal didn't rock her boat by demanding unpalatable decisions.

But Hal had no intention of letting her off so lightly. She might look green and fragile tonight, but he had let her sleep, he had cooked for her, and now it was time she gave him the answer he had to have. One way or another he had to get on with his life.

As soon as they had finished, he cleared away the dishes, made some coffee, and steered Belinda relentlessly back to her sofa.

Once again they were seated opposite each other and Hal's eyes were fixed implacably on her face.

'I want an answer, Belinda. I know you said no the first time.' He shrugged and his mouth curled slightly, 'But . . .'

'But you're generously going to allow me another chance?' Belinda's voice dripped sarcasm. It was the only way she knew to put him off, to push back the tide of panic that was rising in her in waves. If she was forced to answer him now it would be the end. And she couldn't face that.

It was too soon. She wasn't ready.

But Hal's gaze pierced her like an arrow going straight for the heart. 'No. I'm giving *us* another chance, Belinda. I want to marry you. Is there any hope you may want to marry me?'

The words had been spoken. She hadn't been able to forestall him, and now there could be no going back.

She stared down at her knees, which were curled up beside her on the sofa. 'I can't, Hal. I love you. But I can't.'

There was a small hole starting in one of the knees of her jeans. And a speck of mud on the leg. She stared at them, mesmerised, unable to raise her head. And there was no sound in the room, only the faint croaking of a frog somewhere way off in the distance.

Hal didn't speak, and after a while even the frog was silent.

At last Belinda could bear it no longer. Slowly, as if her head were being pulled up by the unseen hand of a puppet-master, she raised her eyes until they encountered his.

And then, although she desperately wanted to, she found she was unable to look away.

It wasn't that his face registered any emotion. It didn't. His mouth was tight, hard, and his eyes were bleak and very still. But it was as if the capacity to feel had left him, and she was looking at what was only a closed and empty shell.

'Hal . . .' she began hesitantly. 'Hal, I'm sorry.'

'No need to be.' Curt. Bored almost. Not as if he cared at all.

Belinda hunched against the arm of the sofa and stared wretchedly at the expressionless mask of his face. She swallowed, and then began again. 'Hal, I don't mean—can't we go on as we have been, at least until—until . . .'

'Until what, Belinda?'

'Until you decide you've—had enough?' Her voice

was so low that it was hardly more than a whisper.

Some sort of emotion did cross his face then and Belinda had a sense that she was stirring passions he was scarcely able to keep under control. 'I've had enough now, Belinda,' he said without inflection. 'You brought something wonderful into my life. Something I hoped might last.' He shrugged, and his lips moved in a caricature of a smile. 'But all good things come to an end, in my experience. Some of them sooner than others.'

'But it doesn't have to end . . .'

'It's already ended.' His tone was so flat and final that she knew it was a waste of breath to try to change his mind.

'Why, Hal?'

'Because you haven't the courage to trust me. Any good partnership is based on trust.'

'I do trust you. It's just that . . .'

'No, Belinda. You don't trust me. I'm not sure you even trust yourself. And you're afraid to commit yourself because you're afraid of being hurt. Yes, I know you were hurt once before—but not so terribly badly—and you've used that as an excuse to avoid trusting anyone since. All right, so you've seen marriages fall apart, including your friend Anthea's. Who hasn't? But life's a risk, Belinda. Until I met you I didn't think I'd be able to love again.' Suddenly he leaned towards her, both hands gripped hard on the arms of his chair. 'If I'd had any sense I'd have left for Victoria, Sicamous or Timbuctoo the moment I noticed you that morning in the park. But I didn't leave. Like a damn fool, I took a chance.'

'Why didn't you leave,' she asked dully, 'instead of making me fall in love with you?'

'Some kind of love, Belinda, when you won't give it a chance to grow. When you won't share my life, or let me share in yours. When you just want us to drift along in a rootless, undefined relationship until it wears out and rusts away. Because that's what you expect, isn't it? That I'll tire of you and wander off to pastures new. Or you will.'

'No. No, *I* won't, Hal. I love you.' Her eyes implored him to understand.

'But I will? Thanks for the vote of confidence.' If eyes could look like black ice, then his did now, and she knew there was no hope of his understanding.

'I didn't mean that. I don't know what I meant.'

'I do. You meant *you* can be faithful and true, but that I'm bound to let you down and break your heart.' There was no mistaking his anger now. The icy control snapped and his eyes were blazing at her with a rage that almost lit the room. The next instant he had leapt to his feet and with his fists rammed into his pockets he was pacing up and down like a caged lion bent on vengeance.

'Hal, don't!' Belinda shook her head from side to side and drove her teeth hard into her lower lip. 'Hal, I can't marry you. Maybe I am afraid, but I believe that's just being realistic. I—if . . .' Desperately she sought for words which would stem the tide of his anger, which might somehow help her to hold him . . .

Hal stopped pacing and went to stand with his back to her at the window. When she turned to look at him his head was bent forward and his hands were pressed flat against the sill as he glared silently out into the night.

'Hal?' He didn't answer, and after a minute she went on haltingly, 'Hal, I—maybe we could live together?'

She wasn't really sure if she could do that, it was a

thought she had always brushed firmly to the back of her mind. Not because she believed it was necessarily wrong—for other people—but she wasn't at all sure it was right for her. Basically she wasn't sure if even a semi-permanent arrangement was a good idea and, rather to her own surprise, she found she didn't altogether like the thought of what amounted to an unsanctified marriage. But she had to offer him something. Otherwise she would lose him.

In the end it made no difference. Without even turning around, Hal said, 'No,' in a voice that sliced through the air like a knife.

Belinda slumped lower in her chair. Her suggestion had not changed anything, it had only increased his anger. And she didn't really understand why. He said he loved her, but if that were so why was he now rejecting the compromise she had found it so hard to make? More than that, he sounded as if he wanted to smash her words in her face.

The silence between them grew longer. Not even a clock ticked and, irrelevantly, Belinda began to wish she had got round to winding the one that now sat like a silent time-bomb on the mantel.

Hal was listening to the silence too, and he knew that in order to end it, in order to bring this bittersweet chapter to a close, he would have to give Belinda an explanation. Because of who she was and what circumstances had made her, he believed now that there was no hope for the two of them. And he was bitter, as well as hurt and angry. But if their love was to be more than just a painful memory, then he must conquer his anger, at least until he had told her why, for him, it had to be marriage or nothing.

Slowly he turned to face her, pressing his hands

firmly behind him against the sill.

She was crouched in a corner of the sofa, looking as small and vulnerable as a bedraggled little bird who has fallen out of the nest, and despite the frustration and hurt that were boiling inside him Hal felt something clutch at his throat.

'Belinda,' he began, forcing himself to speak, 'Belinda, you have to understand. I can't just live with you.'

'Why not? Would your mother object?'

Why had she said that? She knew it was uncalled for. Yes, but she was hurting and, whether it was fair or not, she wanted to hurt him back.

Hal closed his eyes briefly. 'That's hitting below the belt, Belinda. And no, as a matter of fact my mother would probably be delighted. You're quiet, you're not blonde, you like animals—and she has always had a fine disregard for convention when it suits her.'

'Oh. Hal, I'm sorry . . .' She held out a beseeching hand.

'Yes, you should be.' He sounded tired now, as he tightened his grip on the sill and raised his head to stare at a picture of a deer on the wall. 'Listen, Belinda, I have a son as well as a mother.'

'Oh,' said Belinda again. 'I see. You mean Jerry would mind.'

'Yes, I think he would. He's a great kid, considering he's grown up without a mother and with a father who has a bad case of itchy feet. But he doesn't need any more uncertainties in his life. He needs a mother—or stepmother—he can love and rely on, who is legally married to his father so she won't up and run away at the drop of a hat.'

'But—his mother was legally married to you, and . . .'

'That's just it,' Hal interrupted harshly. 'She wasn't.'

'What? But I thought . . .'

'Oh, I know what you thought. For Jerry's sake I hope most people do. But I never told you Dolores was my wife. She—wouldn't marry me, you see. It's not something I'm particularly proud of.' His fingers pressed hard into the wood. 'And it's a subject I never discuss.'

Belinda saw lines deepen beside his mouth as he went on in a hard, flat voice, 'I think Dolores always knew that for her I was just a pleasant sexual fling until the novelty wore off—or somebody better came along—and she adamantly refused any suggestion of marriage. She said she wanted our love to remain free and unfettered—so that neither of us would feel tied down. I was very young and crazily in love with her. She was older than I was, and at the time her attitude seemed impressively modern and free-spirited. So of course I went along with it until Jerry was on the way. I don't think Dolores really meant him to happen, but by then it was much too late.'

'Wouldn't she marry you then either?'

'No. She said nothing had changed, and she wasn't letting any whining little brat pin her down. The amazing thing is that she stayed as long as she did. Looking back, I don't think she cared for Jerry at all.' Without intending to, Hal lowered his head until his eyes came to rest on Belinda. He took a long, harsh breath. 'No. Perhaps on second thoughts it wasn't that amazing. I was starting to make money by then, but I suppose my crime lay in not making it fast enough for her. I was eventually upstaged by a financier from Berlin who fancied blondes.'

'Oh, I see. Is that why you said your mother doesn't

like blondes?'

'It has something to do with it. Mother's prejudices are all on a grand scale, and one bad apple can easily turn her against the entire basket.' He smiled, but his eyes were still as distant as a mirage.

'I'm sorry about Dolores,' said Belinda with quiet sincerity.

'Yes, I believe you are. But now you see why I can't ask Jerry to accept another mother who refuses to marry me. He knows about Dolores, of course. I told him, before someone else decided to do it for me. But I can hardly expect him to trust a woman who won't commit herself, can I? However much he likes her. And I know he does like you, Belinda.'

She stared up into his face, trying to read his mind behind the blank inscrutability of his eyes. After almost a minute had passed she said quietly, 'It's not only Jerry, is it Hal? You don't think you could trust me either.'

Hal stared back at her, and his gaze was hard, speculative, without any of the warmth she longed to see.

'I don't know,' he said finally. 'Maybe I *could* trust you. Even if you wouldn't trust me. But that's academic, isn't it? Because I don't have the slightest intention of finding out. For the last time, Belinda—will you marry me?'

'Hal—Hal, *please* . . .' Her hands fluttered helplessly, and she moved her head in a frantic search for some way to make him understand. To make him stay.

'Is that your answer?'

She nodded, unable to speak, and her eyes were as wide and desperate as he had ever seen them.

'All right. I won't distress you by asking again.' For

a moment he stood motionless, watching her. Then, very slowly, he walked towards her, took her hands and pulled her off the sofa.

Now she was facing him, her small hands clasped in his.

For a long time he stood perfectly still, holding her lightly while his eyes moved steadily over her face and figure. Then, very faintly, she heard him draw in his breath as he bent his head and touched his lips to hers, so softly that she thought she must be dreaming.

With a little cry, she pulled her hands from his and grasped his shoulders, pulling him closer. And as if she had loosed a dam, Hal groaned and put his arms around her waist, holding her in a paralysing grip that barely allowed her to breathe. Not that she wanted to breathe, because now he was kissing her so fiercely that her body felt as if it would melt into his and be consumed in an inferno of the senses which threatened to annihilate them both.

His kiss seemed to go on and on, and then, very gradually, the fire began to die down, the savagery to soften. Finally, with one last, almost gentle brush across her lips, he released her.

'Goodbye, Belinda.' His eyes were dark, haggard pools. For a moment longer they lingered on her face and then he turned away from her, as, through a haze of tears, she saw his wide shoulders disappear through the door.

Belinda waited for the slam that was his trademark. When it didn't come, she knew that he had gone for good.

CHAPTER NINE

'WELL Misty. This just isn't good enough, is it?'

The small dog wagged her question-mark tail and looked hopeful. Maybe her mistress was at last going to stop poking around the house like a sickly tortoise, and get moving and take her for a walk. Misty didn't think much of the funeral march either, and Belinda had been playing that repeatedly over the last few days.

A week had passed since Hal had walked out of the door, and in that time, although Belinda had cared for the animals and seen that they were exercised in the garden, she had felt too depressed and lethargic even to think of going further afield.

Joe had come once, taken one look at her pale, peaky face and asked her what damn fool thing she'd done now. When Belinda told him she had refused to marry Hal and that, no, she was *not* going to change her mind, he had stamped off in a huff saying she was a bird-brained little nitwit—and various less printable phrases—and had refused to visit her since.

Now, for the first time in her life, Belinda was beginning to understand what loneliness was. She had been alone before, but never truly lonely. Even when Hal had been in Vancouver and she had thought he was engaged to Shelagh Devine, there had still been a vague hope hovering at the back of her mind. And of course then she had not known what it was to be loved, to belong heart, soul and body to one man—as Hal, for a brief time, had wholly belonged to her. She missed his love and his closeness more than she would ever have believed possible.

Hal had not come near her again, as she had known he wouldn't, and gradually, now that the die was cast and she was experiencing the reality of an emptiness that would go on forever, she began to wonder if maybe—just maybe—she might have made a mistake.

Ever since she was a small child listening to her father, her life had been geared towards the idea that she would never marry. It had always seemed a fine and practical decision, based squarely on a foundation of common sense.

Now her deep unhappiness and an appalling sense of the futility of a life without Hal were at last beginning to raise doubts in her mind.

Certainly Hal's reasons for insisting on marriage were the right ones for him—and for Jerry. And he did love her, of that she was quite sure.

All at once, as she stood in the kitchen and stared down into Misty's expressive eyes, she made a discovery.

She had to see Hal again. Not tomorrow, not some time, but now.

Twenty minutes later Joe arrived in response to her phone call, muttering that it was about time she started to use what was left of her brain. Five minutes after that she was reversing into the lane as Joe and a disgruntled Misty stood side by side on the step and watched her go.

'Is Mr Blake in?'

Belinda, in jeans and a pink T-shirt, stood at the counter of Blake's Bicycles and looked anxiously up at a stocky young man who was glaring disgustedly at the cash register.

'Hm? Mr Blake? No, I'm afraid he's not.' When Belinda continued to stare at him with a peculiarly desperate look, he added glumly, 'I wish he were. He's the one who programmed this ugly machine, and there's a glitch in it.'

'Oh, dear. What a nuisance,' responded Belinda automatically She looked vaguely around the store and noticed that there were far more bicycles on display than there had been the last time she was in the shop, not to mention shelves full of cycling clothes and accessories. Through the door to the back of the shop she caught a glimpse of a beehive of activity as a gang of busy mechanics worked their way through a stack of repairs and assemblies. Evidently Hal's business in Cinnamon Bay was doing very well, as she had heard Blake's enterprises almost inevitably did.

But where was he? The husky young man was still pushing irritably at the cash register, ignoring her. Belinda decided to try again.

'When will he be back,' she persisted.

'Back? Who?' He looked up, faintly puzzled.

'Mr Blake, of course.'

'Oh. Yes, I didn't explain, did I? Mr Blake has gone down to Victoria.'

Her heart sank. 'Oh, I see. But when do you expect him back?'

'We don't. Not for a while. He says everything's running smoothly up this way—which it would be if I could get this damn drawer open—so he's thinking of opening a new store in the Interior. His house here is back on the market.' When Belinda could only gape at him as a feeling of utter desolation made her heart contract so painfully she thought she was going to keel over, he went on obligingly, 'But at the moment he's still in Victoria, I believe. Perhaps I can help you instead.' He grinned. 'As long as you don't want to buy anything, we're in business. Right now I can't seem to accept your money.' He slammed the flat of his hand down on the cash register.

'No. No, thank you. It's all right. My business was—personal.'

'Oh.' The young man looked at her white face, and said suddenly, 'Look, if it's important, I can probably get a message to him some time.'

She shook her head. 'That's kind of you, but no thanks. I'll—I'll get in touch with him myself.

'Right you are. Sorry I couldn't help you.'

'That's all right.' Belinda moved at a snail's pace to the door and as she reached it she heard the cash register drawer click open and the young man give a grunt of triumph.

She stared down the street, hardly aware of where she was, let alone where she was going. Then suddenly she caught sight of a black cat darting across the road.

When wheels screeched on the tarmac and the animal narrowly escaped being run over, Belinda's drooping figure straightened slowly. The cat had made it. Perhaps that was a good omen for her.

She had wanted to see Hal just to—well, just to see him. But he had gone. All right, so things would not be as simple as she had thought. Still, the situation wasn't hopeless, and if she was going to follow him to Victoria, as she was beginning to suspect she was, it would mean making arrangements for the animals, packing, making decisions . . . Right. But was she really going to go to all that trouble just on some careless whim?

It's not a whim, you idiot, she muttered to herself, as a bolt of understanding seemed to flash down on her out of the sky. Of course it's not. You *need* to see Hal, to be with him, and it's much, much, more than a whim. He's the other half of yourself. Don't you know that without him you can never be whole again?

'You all right, miss?' asked a tourist in Bermuda shorts, scratching nervously at his hairy belly as he passed.

'Yes. Yes, I'm fine.'

Why, oh, why had she had to lose Hal before she was able to face the truth? She loved him, she wanted to be with him for the rest of her life, and there was really no good reason for not marrying. Only her own prejudice. And blindness and obstinacy, she heard a voice, which sounded remarkably like Joe's, murmur inside her head.

I know, she answered the voice. No need to rub it in. I've been a fool. But Hal was wrong about me. I'm not afraid to take risks. Not any more.

The tourist stared at her in alarm, and she realised she was mumbling out loud. Better get moving before he called the local strait-jacket crew.

For a moment longer she hesitated, and then climbing back into her truck she nodded briskly at nothing in particular and took off rather too fast down the street.

Ten minutes later she was pulling up in front of the cottage and Joe and Misty were watching her as if they hadn't moved since she left.

'Of course you ought to go, girl,' Joe snorted, as they sat at their usual places at the table, holding their usual cups of coffee.

'I know. I'm going to do it anyway, but I guess I just want someone to tell me it's the right thing, and that I'm not making a fool of myself.'

'Huh. It's the first intelligent idea you've had for weeks. You've been a fool for long enough, Bella.'

'I suppose I have. But you see—well, Dad brought

me up not to think of marriage and then there was Anthea and—oh, other things—and of course my father left my mother . . .'

'What?' Joe interrupted loudly. 'What are you talking about, girl?'

'Dad leaving Mother. You know . . .'

'But he didn't.' Heavy grey eyebrows beetled alarmingly and Belinda sank back against her chair. Joe's deep-set eyes continued to glare at her, and then he asked fiercely, 'Did my old friend Steven tell you that?'

'Yes. Yes, he did. Isn't it . . .?'

'No, of course it isn't true.' Joe was shouting now. 'The old fraud. I knew your parents when they were still living in a shack down the highway, and believe me, your Dad was crazy about your mother right up until the day she died.'

'But I don't understand. He always said they got married because I was coming, and that it had been a terrible mistake, because my mother changed after that and thought she owned him. He said that in the end she got so hard to live with that he took me with him and left.'

'Rubbish. They got married because *he* wanted it. And your mother didn't change. She was a lovely lady. But Steven was something else. He'd always been a selfish bastard, but over the years he got worse. Impossibly demanding and possessive. It wasn't marriage that forced your parents apart, Bella. It was Steven. In the end your unfortunate mother just couldn't take him any more. I'm sure she still loved him for some reason, but still, she couldn't take it. Besides, she had you to consider. So she left. Don't blame her. People could hear him shouting at her from half a mile away.'

Joe picked up his cup and then banged it down on the

table without drinking. 'And don't you believe that story about him taking you away, either,' he went on irascibly. 'He didn't. Your mother only sent you back to Steven because she knew she was dying. He tried to see her again then, of course, but he arrived too late.' Joe's lined face twisted in a grimace of reluctant compassion. 'That didn't improve his disposition either. Anyway, it was then that he moved into this place.' He stared ruminatively out of the window. 'But of course you'd be too young to remember.'

'Yes. Yes, I would. I always thought Mother didn't want me. All these years—Joe, why would Father tell me lies like that?'

Joe sighed noisily. 'I suppose he lied to save his pride. He was a stubborn man, my friend Steven, and he had a lot of pride. I guess he didn't want his daughter to think he couldn't hold on to a woman. He was a bitter old misery by then, but he loved you in his own distorted way. Wanted you to think well of him.'

'I know. I lived with him. And sometimes he was—quite kind.' Belinda stirred her cold coffee thoughtfully. 'I'm glad you told me, Joe.'

'Huh. Would have told you before. Thought you knew.'

'No. No, I didn't. But—oh, I *am* glad my mother wanted me. And that it wasn't just getting married that broke up my parents.'

Joe glanced at her suspiciously. 'Why? Should have thought what I've said about your father would make you even more suspicious of my sex. No good pretending he treated that lovely woman well. Because he didn't.'

'I know, but you see—well, Hal's not like my father. I know that now. He thinks I don't trust him, but I do.

I—I guess it was partly myself I didn't trust, and I was afraid that if we got married . . . Oh Joe, I don't know *what* I thought.'

'Didn't think at all, if you ask me,' muttered Joe.

Belinda smiled sheepishly. 'You may be right. But I'm thinking now, and I'm not afraid to take a chance. In fact it won't even be a chance because I know that, if Hal can ever manage to forgive me, then everything will just have to be all right. What you've told me only makes me more certain.' She paused, and added slowly, 'Joe, do you think he will forgive me?'

'Don't know. Obstinate man too, that one. Likes his own way. But *he's* not a fool.' His eyes twinkled at her. 'Worth a try, I'd say.'

Yes, it's certainly worth a try, thought Belinda the next day, as she sat in one of the two cars of the old E & N Railway and watched the scenery speed past the tree-lined track to Victoria.

But by the time the train reached the Johnson Street Terminal her heart was pounding like a maddeningly persistent hammer, and her mind was going round in circles trying to find something to worry about besides what she would say to Hal.

For a moment she did manage a small fuss about how Joe and Jack would cope with the animals in her absence, but that didn't last long because she knew perfectly well they had never had any problems with her menagerie in the past.

Almost at once her thoughts flew back to Hal.

As Belinda hoisted her one light bag on to her shoulder and stepped down on to the platform she remembered that in all the flurry of departure, she had not even thought about booking herself a room. She sighed. She supposed she could start calling frantically from the nearest phone booth, but it was June, the tourist season was in full swing, and anyway she only had one quarter. That left her with little alternative but to cast herself on the mercy of a taxi driver.

Luckily for her, the taxi driver had daughters of his own, and after one look at her white and worried face he said that what she needed was not some fancy hotel, but a nice bed and breakfast with a proprietor who would give her a solid meal.

Belinda gave him a watery smile and said yes, that would be perfect.

Half an hour later she was settled into a bright single room with old-fashioned, serviceable furniture, not far from Beacon Hill Park.

Right, she thought, thumping herself down in a large and lumpy leather chair. Now what?

She glanced at her watch. Nearly six o'clock. Blake's Bicycles would be closed. She knew Hal's mother lived somewhere in Oak Bay and that if Hal was not enjoying one of his 'private' visits to his flat, he would probably be staying with his family—assuming of course that his manager in Cinnamon Bay had any real idea what his boss was doing, which was by no means certain.

Belinda wandered out into the hall and picked up the telephone book. Blair . . . Blais . . . Blake . . . Oh, dear. There were an awful lot of them. But as Hal owned the house his mother lived in, perhaps it would be listed under his name.

It wasn't, but there was only one H. Blake in the area where she knew the house to be. She jotted down a blurred but readable address on a piece of pink tissue which was all the paper she had to hand. Then she stared at the phone. Should she?

No. No, she had to *see* him. That way he couldn't

hang up on her. That last goodbye of his had been so—final.

Later it occurred to her that she should have remembered that although he couldn't hang up on her in person, there were other ways of dismissing last week's lovers.

She went back to her room and gazed thoughtfully at the meagre supply of clothes which she had brought with her.

Jeans, no track-suits, two T-shirts and a bright red blouse. Oh, dear. She hadn't packed the red striped skirt that was supposed to go with the blouse. She had bought them especially to please Hal, and he had never even seen them. She glared morosely at an unaccommodating drawer, but it yielded up no magical apparition of red stripes.

Frowning, she settled resignedly for jeans, and tucked the blouse carefully inside the waistband.

Could be worse, she decided, surveying herself in the mirror. Figure quite trim, and that colour does brighten up your face, Belinda Ballantyne. Hal had been irritatingly right about her taste in clothes.

Finally, after a moment's hesitation, she returned to the drawer, took out a box and then slipped on the bracelet Hal had given her. Jeans and diamonds! She smiled to herself. Well, so what? If there had ever been an occasion when she needed the morale-boost of diamonds, then this was it.

A few minutes later she took a deep breath and went to call another taxi.

The house she was almost sure was Hal's was a large, older building with an unusual amount of brickwork for this part of the world. It was three storeys high, set in spacious grounds and surrounded by intimidatingly well-cut lawns. Belinda thought of her own casual attempts at gardening and groaned inwardly. Beyond the house she could see trees, and between the gently waving branches there was a glimpse of blue where the grounds dipped down sharply to the waters of the bay.

She glanced at her clean but inelegant jeans, and wrinkled her nose in resignation. Maybe she didn't exactly fit into these opulent surroundings—but there was nothing she could do about that and she certainly hadn't come this far to be defeated by a rather large house with a stunningly well kept garden.

With a determined tilt to her chin, Belinda paid off the driver and marched down the evenly paved path towards her future.

For a long time after she rang the bell no one answered. She was about to ring again when suddenly the door was jerked open by a stout, panting woman in an apron, with fuzzy grey hair and eyes that popped like a frog's.

'Oh, I'm sorry,' began Belinda. 'I didn't mean to interrupt you . . .'

The woman shook her head, still panting, and looking more like a hairy frog than ever. 'S'all right,' she gasped. 'You caught me with my hands in the sink, love, so I had to dry them first.'

'Yes, of course. You must be Hattie. Is—is Mr Blake in?'

Just then Belinda caught a movement at the back of the hallway, and before she even had time to take a breath, a well-remembered voice said, 'I'll take care of it, Hattie,' and she found herself staring up into Hal's carved-stone face, as Hattie, with another little puff, bustled busily back to her sink.

His hand was gripped tightly round the doorknob

which he had wrested almost rudely from the housekeeper's grasp, and he was glaring down at Belinda with his lips rigidly compressed and his face darkened by a seething fury that froze the words in her throat.

Surely this was not the man she had come to find? The man she loved? And yet—yes, when she looked closely, she saw a reflection in his eyes of emotions which matched her own. For they were deeper than ever, the lines around them more pronounced. He looked gaunt and exhausted—and yet quite gloweringly sexual and attractive.

At least that hadn't changed.

Hal was wearing hip-hugging, fawn-coloured slacks and he must have been in the process of getting dressed, for although his pale cream shirt was pushed into his belt, only half of it was buttoned, and his cuffs hung open at the wrists. His feet, she noticed, were invitingly brown and bare. And every inch of him exuded masculinity, sensuality—and rejection. Only his eyes revealed that this glorious male animal who could reduce her to melting imbecility at a glace was not the arrogant and unfeeling master of all mortal emotions, but a man with a heart which endured a torment as great as any she had known, or greater.

'Hal . . .' She stretched out her hand to the tall, unmoving statue in the doorway. He stared down at it, raised his eyes to flick, rapier-like, over her body and then, with a quick, cruel twist of his lips, he slammed the door violently in her face.

It was only as the reverberations died quietly away across the garden that she remembered there were more ways than one to dismiss lovers who were no longer loved.

CHAPTER TEN

FOR an endless moment Belinda stood still, riveted to the step and totally incapable of moving. Her eyes were fixed on the lock of the door and she seemed unable to tear them away.

Was this the end? She supposed it must be. So, for all Hal's protestations of love, it had taken him only one week to decide that whatever he felt about her was over, and that he didn't want to see her any more.

Very slowly, the shock which had frozen her to the step began to wear off, and she felt the beginnings of an anger which threatened to rival his.

All right, so she had behaved like the dimwit Joe had called her. She had hurt him. But if he loved her at all, as he'd said he did, he had no right to slam the door in her face. No right to treat her as if she were a bothersome pedlar trying to unload a case of sour apples or some patent religion that came by post. It would not have hurt him to talk to her even if, in the end, he still insisted it was finished between them.

Her chin lifted indignantly and she raised her hand to pound it on the door. But just before her fist hit the wood she thought better of it. She wouldn't give him the satisfaction of making her grovel. Because that was how he would interpret any further attempt to gain admittance.

She would leave with quiet dignity, she decided, because, knowing Hal as she did, he would be watching.

With her shoulders straight and her head held high, she walked slowly away down the path.

She had almost reached the low white gate when a voice so filled with pain that she barely recognised it shouted, 'Belinda! Wait.'

Belinda paused for a moment, then remembered Hal's cruelly twisted face as he slammed the door on her.

She continued her sedate march to the gate.

Her fingers were on the latch when she felt the hand on her shoulder, and then she didn't feel anything except the singing between her ears. Hal had swung her round dizzyingly fast, but that was not what made her head spin. When her vision cleared, and she saw his face, the love in his eyes was so palpable that it nearly knocked her off her feet.

'Belinda, I'm sorry. Can you forgive me?'

All at once the anger which had sustained her on her slow progress to the gate evaporated into the air as though it had never been. And she saw only the face of the man she loved, strong, more worn than she remembered, but filled with a passionate tenderness—and a remorse that broke her heart.

'There's nothing to forgive, Hal. Not really.'

'Yes, there is.' His fingers dug unconsciously into her shoulders, trying to emphasise what he so desperately needed to make her understand. 'Belinda, I love you. This past week has been hell on earth, and the only way I could cope with it was rage. I've been thinking black thoughts of you for seven days now, hoping you were as miserable as I was. And when I saw your pert little face in the doorway, all wide-eyed and sweet and beseeching, all I could think of was the rack you'd put me through, and for just that disastrous split second I wanted to put you through it too. So I slammed the door on my dreams.' His lips curved in a smile that was more of a grimace. Then his eyes fell on the diamond bracelet and the smile turned soft with love. 'Can you understand that, Belinda?'

'Yes,' said Belinda, 'I can. Because the same kind of rage got me down this path—and stopped me from turning back when you called. Shouted, actually.' She glanced wryly at the hands grasping her shoulders. 'All the same, Hal, I think my understanding would be greatly assisted if you left me with some feeling in my arms.'

'What? Oh, good lord. Belinda, I'm sorry. I didn't even realise . . .' His hands dropped abruptly and came to rest on her waist.

A tall gentleman in tweeds passing in the road with his dog peered over the gate and remarked testily that the standards of public behaviour in this neighbourhood were deteriorating quite disgracefully.

'Oh, dear,' said Belinda. 'Have I got you into trouble with the local morality squad?'

'No,' replied Hal. 'You haven't. I make my own trouble, young lady. Like this.'

Suddenly his arms snaked around her waist and she found herself pulled hard against his chest. And then all awareness of morality squads, and the public in general, was wiped from both their minds as his lips found hers and they swayed together in an embrace which made a mockery of all the desolate days they had spent apart.

When they finally drew away from each other, Hal's shirt was hanging loose over his slacks and Belinda's red blouse was undone half-way.

'Oh, dear,' she said again. 'You do look sexy, Hal, but I have a feeling that's not *quite* the sort of image this neighbourhood likes to promote.'

'Oh, I don't know.' Hal grinned at her. 'I think I add

a certain tone to it, don't you?'

'Definitely,' she replied with feeling. 'A gloriously sexy tone.'

'Porcupine.' Hal's arms circled her again and he held her loosely, his hands brushing erotically over her lower back. 'Belinda . . .'

'Mm?' she murmured, her cheek pressed dreamily against his bare brown chest.

'Belinda, I don't know why you're here. But I meant it when I said I wouldn't ask you to marry me again.'

'I know. I'm here because I love you Hal. I've been a complete idiot. And if you won't ask me again—then I guess I'll just have to think of something else.'

With a mischievous little grin, she wriggled out of his arms, and before Hal realised what she was about she had gone down on one knee in front of him, and was taking his large hand in her small one.

'I love you, Hal Blake,' she said with a sincerity that was not greatly belied by the impish gleam in her eyes. 'I love you, and I always will, because you're strong and kind and you make me laugh, and—and—oh, just because I do. Will you marry me, Hal? Please.'

Her voice was brimming with laughter as well as love and Hal, grinning down at her, said, 'Oh, shut up, you adorable fool,' and pulled her up into his arms.

The tweedy gentleman with the dog, returning from his walk, passed the gate again at that moment and this time was rendered quite speechless.

'Hmm,' said Belinda several minutes later. 'Is that the way you reply to a lady's proposal? By telling her to shut up, and then calling her a fool?'

'Invariably,' replied Hal imperturbably. 'By the way, in that thoroughly commendable catalogue you just made of my many virtues, you left out the most important thing.'

'What's that?' asked Belinda suspiciously.

'That I make love to you with tireless dedication, flair, originality, sophistication . . .'

'And an exceedingly swelled head,' interrupted Belinda dampingly. 'Granted that some of the above may be true—it really isn't the most important thing, Hal.'

Hal laughed, the expression in his eyes very tender. 'I know I love you, my Belinda. And I'll marry you if you'll marry me.'

'Oh, Hal. I'm so happy.'

'So am I.'

His hands were already on her waist, and in a moment they would have slipped around her back, if a penetrating voice had not called from an open window, 'Harold! Jerry and I have enjoyed this touching reunion immensely. But now I think you've entertained us long enough.'

The lovers leaped apart as if they had been stung by a swarm of militant bees.

'Ah,' said Hal. 'Mother. I wondered when we'd be hearing from that department.' He raised an arm and waved casually at the window.

Belinda gasped. 'Hal! Do you mean to tell me you knew your mother was watching?'

'The possibility had crossed my mind.'

'But—but—oh, Hal, how could you? She's never even met me, and now she'll think I'm a—a . . .'

'Floozy? Wanton woman? Lady of dubious virtue?' suggested Hal hopefully. 'In that case, I sincerely hope she's right.'

His lack of concern infuriated Belinda, who felt that meeting his mother for the first time wearing blue jeans was disadvantage enough.

'Yes,' she wailed. 'All of the above and then some. Hal, you had no business . . .'

'No business to what?'

'To make love to me in front of your mother and Jerry.'

'Hattie too, unless I'm very much mistaken,' remarked Hal with equanimity. 'She's been with us for thirty years, and she thinks anything my family does is as much her business as ours. But I wasn't actually making love to you, Belinda. Unfortunately.'

'That doesn't make me feel any better,' replied Belinda in a small, choked voice.

Hal glanced down at the top of her bent, curly head. Then he put a finger beneath her chin and lifted it. When he saw that she was genuinely distressed, he was immediately and devastatingly contrite.

'Belinda, love, I was only teasing. Mother won't hold it against you. As she said, she was vastly entertained—and in any case, if she held it against anyone, I assure you it would be me. My mother, I very much regret to say, is firmly convinced I can do no right. She's been disapproving of me for so long it'll probably quite ruin her day to discover that I'm finally going to do something she wants.'

'What does she want?' asked Belinda doubtfully.

'She wants me to get married to a nice girl who will keep me in order—which I suspect means in Victoria—and who will produce a few nice granddaughters for her. She says the Blake men make too much noise and never do what they're told.' He grinned unrepentantly.

'I expect she's right.'

'Of course she is. I told you before you two would

get on like a house on fire.'

'Mm.' Belinda was still dubious. 'Hal?'

'Yes, love?' He put an arm around her waist, turned to look up at the house, and discreetly began to fasten up the buttons at her back.

'Those granddaughters—do you want them?'

'Certainly. But only if they look like you.' He smiled down at her with so much love and warmth in his eyes that Belinda thought her heart would burst in two. And she realised for the first time that in all those years when she had been determined to maintain her single state, she had never once considered that she would be giving up the chance to have children. Now she didn't have to consider it, and she was glad. She smiled back at Hal, her small face radiant with love, and completely forgetting about the watchers in the window.

But Hal hadn't forgotten. Suddenly he pulled Belinda to his side, lifted his head and shouted into the air, 'It's all right, Mother. We're getting married. And you're in luck. Belinda wants granddaughters too.'

'Hal!' remonstrated Belinda. 'Behave yourself.' She tried desperately to control her laughter, and then gave up. 'You're impossible,' she groaned, recovering her breath with difficulty. 'If your mother expects me to keep you in order, I'm afraid she's in for a sad disappointment.'

'So are you, if you try it, my love.'

Belinda was just opening her mouth to make a sharp retort, when that voice which was almost as carrying as Hal's called acidly, 'I'm sure the neighbours are as delighted to hear that news as I am, Harold. And now perhaps we could discuss the details in private.'

'Yes, Mother,' Hal shouted back with suspicious meekness. 'Whatever you say.' In a lower voice he murmured to Belinda, 'Come on, love. The stars must be in perfect alignment today. Mother's in an exceptionally mellow mood.'

'Harold.' Mrs Blake's voice rose threateningly. 'You come inside this minute.'

'Hmm. I take it back about the stars,' Hal muttered. Then he added reminiscently, 'How I used to dread those words when I was a boy. They invariably presaged a very unpleasant ten minutes.'

'I expect it served you right,' replied Belinda unsympathetically.

'Heartless wench. It did, as a matter of fact. I wouldn't have wanted the job of raising me.'

'Harold . . .' Mrs Blake's voice rose again.

'Coming, Mother.' He started to lead Belinda towards the house, and then bending down whispered into her ear, 'Don't worry, love. She'll adore you.'

Belinda was by no means convinced, but she was given no chance to hang back as Hal drew her inexorably towards the big front door.

A second later it was flung open to reveal a tall, white-haired woman who was standing beside Jerry in the hallway. No, Belinda corrected herself at once, taking in the regal bearing, patrician features and smartly elegant black dress. Not woman. Lady. Very much so.

'Mother, this is Belinda,' said Hal, announcing the obvious as if he had just pulled a rabbit out of a hat.

'I see,' replied Mrs Blake severely, eyeing her guest over the top of a pair of silver-framed glasses. 'The one who wants granddaughters, as you have just informed most of Oak Bay.'

Was there a glint of humour in the corner of the steel-grey eyes? Belinda wasn't sure.

'Well, daughters first,' she said hurriedly. 'But of course they'd be your granddaughters, wouldn't they, Mrs Blake? Or grandsons.'

Mrs Blake shook her head. 'Granddaughters,' she said firmly. 'Gerald and my son are quite sufficient trouble to be going on with. Do come in, Miss . . .?'

'Ballantyne. Belinda.'

'Ah. Yes, Belinda, of course. But I do think it's always an advantage to know the last names of prospective daughters-in-law, don't you?' She shot Hal an accusing look and turned to lead the way into the house, adding over her shoulder, 'My son doesn't agree with me, naturally. He has a very trying habit of introducing underdressed young women merely as Jeanie or Melissa or Diane. But then perhaps it's not important, as they always disappear without trace.'

'Belinda's not going to disappear, Mother,' Hal assured her solemnly. Only a slight quiver at the corner of his mouth betrayed the effort it was costing him to keep his face straight.

'Possibly not,' retorted Mrs Blake. 'And at least she's not a blonde.'

'Belinda's terrific, Grandma,' interposed Jerry, who up until now had been uncharacteristically quiet. 'She looks after animals. And snakes.'

'Not any more she doesn't,' muttered Hal under his breath.

'Oh, yes, I do,' contradicted Belinda in an equally low voice. 'At least, I'll concede the snakes, but I'm not going to live without animals.'

'Done,' said Hal promptly. 'It's a deal.'

Belinda didn't respond, because she was busy admiring the large panelled hallway with its beautifully polished wood floor, and taking in the collection of

Victorian oils which lined the walls. Her friend Joe would be enchanted, she decided. For some reason he particularly admired Victorian art.

Mrs Blake led them to a bright, cheerful sitting-room at the back of the house overlooking the gardens. Here the paintings were mostly of birds and dogs, but Belinda, who had been well schooled by Joe, saw at once that these were much more than just pretty, decorative pictures.

As Mrs Blake sat down in a high-backed chair which bore a remarkable resemblance to a throne, Hal guided Belinda to a love-seat and then settled himself beside her.

'Belinda is admiring your paintings, Mother,' said Hal, who had been quietly observing the woman who had come back to him when he had all but given up hope.

Mrs Blake looked at her sharply. 'In that case you have an eye for beauty, my dear.'

'Oh. Thank you.' Belinda was startled by the unexpected accolade. 'Your pictures are beautiful, Mrs Blake.'

'Belinda also has your deplorable taste in music, Mother,' Hal continued with exaggerated gloom.

'*And* she looks after all kinds of animals,' put in Jerry, who was sitting in a window seat and fidgeting with the curtains. 'Grandma has two poodles and two cats,' he told Belinda with satisfaction.

'Yes,' said Mrs Blake. 'But at the moment they're in the garden—no doubt digging up my rutabagas. I'm glad you like animals and music, Belinda. It's more than I can say for my son.'

'I like animals,' objected Hal.

'I was referring to music, Harold,' Mrs Blake said

repressively. 'And please don't tell me that you like music too. That caterwauling you listen to is *not* music.'

'I like U2 and Whitesnake,' remarked Jerry, grinning provocatively at his grandmother.

'And *that* we won't even discuss, Gerald,' replied Mrs Blake with a quelling glare. She caught Belinda's eye and they exchanged a glance of complete understanding.

Belinda, sighing inwardly with relief, relaxed and sank back against the cushions. Hal's mother was a character sure enough. But Hal was right. They were going to get along like a house on fire. And the blue jeans didn't matter at all.

'Now,' said Mrs Blake, folding her hands in her lap and fixing a steely eye on her son. 'When do you propose to get married?'

'Tomorrow?' suggested Hal.

'Don't be ridiculous. We'll settle for an August wedding, I think. At the Cathedral . . .'

'No, we won't,' said Hal. 'We'll settle for a June wedding. A small one. At St Mark's.'

'Perhaps we could compromise?' Belinda's eyes glanced from one stubborn face to the other. 'Maybe a July wedding . . .'

'At the Cathedral,' said Mrs Blake intractably.

Hal sighed. 'All right. I accept defeat.' He slapped his hands down on his thighs and stood up. 'Belinda, let's go for a walk.'

'You are not going anywhere, Harold,' said Mrs Blake forcefully. 'We are discussing your wedding at the moment.'

'We'll discuss it another time, Mother. Now I want to be alone with Belinda.'

'In view of the fact that you're only half dressed, I

hardly think that will be suitable,' replied his mother. 'I hope you don't propose to sit down to dinner in that semi-nude state, Harold. And there will be plenty of time to be alone with Belinda when you're married.'

'Yes, Hal,' agreed Belinda quickly. 'We can go for a walk later on. But as I've only just met your mother, I do think we have a lot to talk about.'

'I knew it,' muttered Hal, lowering himself beside her again with bad grace, and fastening his cuffs with a jerk. 'It's a conspiracy.'

'Yeah, Grandma and Belinda against us, Dad,' chipped in Jerry from the window.

'Precisely what I'm afraid of,' agreed Hal, turning a bleak eye on his son.

'You're exactly what Harold needs, Belinda,' said Mrs Blake, ignoring him. 'And I'm delighted you changed your mind about getting married. He told me about that. Or rather I dragged it out of him. He's been exceedingly hard to live with this past week.'

'I am never hard to live with,' said Hal self-righteously.

'Really? Well, I'm afraid if you think I find your pacing up and down all night, hitting the walls with your fist and using the most atrocious language, amusing, then you are very much mistaken,' his mother informed him tartly.

'Was I that bad?'

'Yeah, and you drove the car through the back hedge too, Dad, and broke three squash rackets . . .'

'That will do, Gerald. But I quite agree. Your father has *not* been behaving at all well.'

Hal put an arm around Belinda's shoulders and smiled down at her. 'Will you still marry me, love?' he asked, laughing into her eyes. 'After that glowing testimonial from my loyal family, I really don't see how you can refuse.'

'Neither do I,' replied Belinda happily, resting her head on his arm. 'The prospect is quite irresistible.'

Four weeks later—in July—Hal and Belinda were married, not in the Cathedral and not at St Mark's, but at the little church in Cinnamon Bay which Belinda had attended off and on all her life.

This reversal of Mrs Blake's carefully laid plans for a large and very social wedding had come about because Belinda had tactfully persuaded Hal's mother that as she had no family to invite, it would be very awkward if the bride's side of the church was almost empty. She suggested that if the wedding were held in Cinnamon Bay, Belinda's schoolfriends would attend, along with friends of the Blakes who could make the journey up from Victoria. Eventually Mrs Blake had conceded that this arrangement was, in the circumstances, entirely appropriate.

Hal had been delighted at this toning down of his mother's grandiose schemes, and immediately suggested that, since Belinda had been so successful at winning her point, perhaps she could also arrange to have the wedding held in June, preferably the next day.

But on this Belinda had been adamant. She said Mrs Blake was entitled to reasonable consideration, and time to make her arrangements. Hal said that, as his mother had been arranging him all his life, this time he wanted things his way. Which meant now.

'You always have things your way,' Belinda reminded him. 'But as you can't get married without a bride, this time you'll just have to wait.'

Reluctantly, Hal had been obliged to give in.

Now, at last, the wedding was over. Hal's best man, an old schoolfriend, had left to catch the ferry with Anthea, who had returned briefly from Toronto to be Belinda's bridesmaid. Joe, of course, had given her away, looking remarkably spruce in a new pin-striped grey suit. Much to the bride and groom's glee, he had hit it off so well with Mrs Blake that Hal had been moved to suggest that wedding bells in that quarter were not unlikely.

'Mm,' said Belinda thoughtfully. 'Joe's a rough diamond, but he does have some cultured edges . . .'

'And mother's a cultured pearl with an appreciation for diamonds, rough or smooth.' Hal grinned. 'They're made for each other.'

Belinda gazed up at her husband of half an hour and wondered if he was right. She didn't want her old friend Joe to be lonely when she moved away. He wouldn't like not having anyone to grumble at. On the other hand, she couldn't see him surrendering to the cosy comfort of Victoria either. Still, no doubt things would take their course . . .

As they sat in the kitchen of the cottage, happily exhausted and glad to be alone, Hal raised his glass. 'To my beautiful bride,' he said softly.

'To my handsome husband,' she replied. And then, her dark eyes shining with happiness, 'To us.'

'To us.' Hal put down his glass and added feelingly, 'These past two weeks have been one hell of a strain, Belinda.'

'I don't see why,' she said, pretending not to understand him.

'Have you any idea what it's been like living in the same house with you, but with Mother monitoring my every move so closely that I barely had a chance to lay a hand on you, let alone anything else?'

'Yes,' said Belinda, trying to look demure and not succeeding. 'As a matter of fact I have a very good idea. She was monitoring my every move too, remember.'

'How could I forget?'

Belinda laughed, and didn't answer as her mind ran back over the last few chaotic weeks.

In the first place, as soon as they had settled on a date, she had returned to Cinnamon Bay to make arrangements for the wedding and also to relieve Joe and Jack of the job of looking after the animals. When she checked her reservations book she was relieved to discover that she had no bookings after the middle of July, so there would be no difficulty in winding up her business.

Because wind it up she would have to. Mrs Blake, with magnanimous and thoroughly autocratic insistence, had told them that she had reached a time in her life when she wished to move to a more central and self-contained location where she could end her days being looked after by the staff of a luxurious retirement residence. The house in Oak Bay, she told her son and future daughter-in-law in a voice which brooked no argument, would henceforth be their responsibility. So would the dogs, the rutabagas and Hattie.

Hal, his eyes gleaming with amused gratitude, had at first been inclined to remonstrate, but then common sense had taken over and he had realised that his mother, for once, might actually be making sense. He had then, with an arrogance which rivalled Mrs Blake's, informed Belinda that she had better sell her cottage in Cinnamon Bay.

Belinda refused point-blank. She said she had lived in the cottage all her life and that, although she was delighted at the thought of moving to Victoria, she had no intention of severing all her ties with her home town.

'I'll be back at least once a year, if only to get away from you,' she told Hal pointedly. There were times when she felt his dictatorial ways needed some sort of setback.

'Well, of course you can keep your house if you want to,' he replied with benevolent arrogance. Then he grinned provocatively. 'Although you'll never want to get away from me, Belinda.'

'How generous of you. And don't be too sure,' she muttered.

All the same, she suspected he was right, because after she had concluded her business in Cinnamon Bay and returned to Victoria she had found the discretion necessitated by Mrs Blake's eagle-eyed surveillance quite as much of a strain on her as Hal complained it was on him.

As she looked across the table at him now, leaning back with his shirt open, his sleeves rolled up and his dark eyes fixed on her in seductive appreciation, she couldn't really imagine wanting to get away from Hal.

In a moment he stood up, came around to stand beside her chair and then pulled her purposefully into his arms.

'You know, spending our wedding night here wasn't one of your brighter ideas, love,' he murmured into her hair. His hands began to slide deliciously down her spine.

'Yes, it was. It was here that I learned to love you. Where all the dreams I never knew I had came true.'

'A charming sentiment, my love. But there's a problem.'

'What's that?'

'The fact that when I investigated your bedroom a

few minutes ago I discovered one narrow and very virginal-looking bed—which is currently occupied by a dog.'

Belinda smiled and curled her fingers gently around his neck. 'Misty is very susceptible to bribery,' she assured him. 'And as for the other problem, I believe you'll find a solution.'

She was right. He did.

Afterwards, as they lay wrapped in a loving intimacy occasioned partly by their desire to be close to each other, and partly by a disinclination to fall out of bed, Hal whispered into her ear, 'I love you, my Belinda. I can't think of anyone I'd rather spend my life with. But tell me, is there any hope at all that I may one day manage to share a bed with you without first clearing a path through your dogs?'

'I expect so,' said Belinda, rubbing her cheek against his shoulder. 'Misty will undoubtedly be captivated by one of your mother's poodles and desert me for a love nest in the rutabagas.'

'So far so good. And can I take that as an assurance that you're not planning to turn the conservatory into a half-way house for homeless canines, or the basement into a hostel for stray cats?'

'Yes,' she replied confidently. 'You can. Because I've already found a job with the local vet, so I won't have time to run a boarding-kennel any longer.'

'You've what?' Hal sat up so abruptly that Belinda landed in a pink and undignified heap on the floor.

'Oh, lord, I'm sorry.' He pulled her up beside him again. 'I didn't mean to start our marriage by throwing you out of bed. What's all this rubbish about a vet?'

'Not rubbish. In all the excitement I just forgot to tell you. I've got a job.'

'Right. Looking after me and Jerry.'

'You, Mr Blake, have done a splendid job of looking after yourself for years. As for Jerry—and the dogs and the rutabagas—I am not a total incompetent. I can handle more than one activity at a time. And besides, there's always Hattie.'

'Hmm.' He stared at her, and for a moment she anticipated a roar of objection, and orders to damn well do what she was told. But instead he smiled suddenly, that magically melting smile that curled her toes. 'Yes,' he agreed with startling equanimity. 'I do believe you're right.' Then the smile turned into a leer as he added meaningfully, 'But for now I'll settle for just one activity. This one.'

Laughing, he pulled her on top of him, and it was quite some time before either of them thought any more about jobs or dogs or cats.

'I've got a present for you,' said Hal much later, when Belinda was at last beginning to drift off to sleep in his arms.

'Mm. Have you? Lovely,' she murmured drowsily. 'What is it?'

'Get up and I'll show you.'

'Now?'

'Sure. Come on. Get up, lazybones.' He tapped her lightly on the bottom and swung his long legs over the side of the bed.

'But it's . . .' She glanced at her watch. 'Three a.m.'

'The perfect time. Now make yourself decent—well, not too decent—and come into the living-room.'

Belinda, deciding that the only way she would get any sleep was to comply, stumbled over to the cupboard to find her robe.

When she reached the living-room, Hal, wearing only

a pair of skin-tight black jeans, was leaning back on the sofa with his legs crossed.

'Come here,' he ordered.

Wondering, Belinda went to sit beside him.

At first he said nothing, but instead sat studying her quietly with an enigmatic smile softening his sensual lips. Smiling back, she put her head on his shoulder and almost at once her eyelids began to droop closed.

'Hey. Wake up.' Hal was shaking her gently as, startled, she looked up into his face.

'Oh,' she murmured, her voice slurred with sleep. 'I must have drifted off. You said you had a present for me, didn't you?' And if he didn't let her have it soon, she thought dreamily, she really would fall asleep, so soundly that she was sure no amount of shaking would waken her.

But then, to her amazement, Hal suddenly sprang to his feet and loped across to her stereo. He stretched out a hand, and a moment later the strains of Schubert's Unfinished Symphony came drifting across the room.

Belinda's eyes snapped open as all thoughts of sleep evaporated. 'Oh,' she gasped. 'Oh, Hal. How did you know . . .?'

'I checked your records, of course,' he told her with smug satisfaction, 'and I saw you didn't have this one. Somehow the Unfinished Symphony seemed—appropriate.'

'Yes,' said Belinda. 'Unfinished. That's us, isn't it?'

'You and I will never be finished, Belinda.' His fingers ran softly down her cheek as he returned to sit beside her.

'Hal . . .?' She hesitated.

'Mm?'

'Thank you. Thank you for giving me Schubert. It's

the nicest thing you've ever done for me.'

'Is it? Why?'

'Because I know you hate it so.'

'I don't hate it. Not when it's a part of you.'

'Dear Hal. I don't hate your music either.'

'That's a dangerous admission, my love.'

'Why do you say that?'

'Because, don't you see, it means the day may yet come when my kind of music is yours.'

'And mine yours?'

He made a face. 'Well, I suppose, for your sake, I could *try* to enjoy it.'

Belinda caught his hand, not sure whether she wanted to laugh or cry. 'Coming from you, Hal, that *is* devotion above and beyond.'

'Yes,' he agreed. 'It is, isn't it? Above and beyond—and forever.'

She knew then that what she wanted to do was kiss him.

As Hal appeared to have the same idea, if Misty had not wandered in at that moment in pursuit of an early breakfast, decided the prospects were not promising and sat on them, they would probably have remained there till morning.

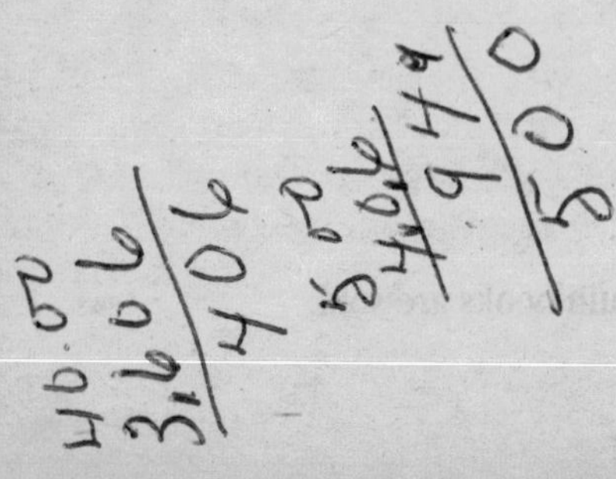

HARLEQUIN'S WISHBOOK
SWEEPSTAKES RULES & REGULATIONS

NO PURCHASE NECESSARY TO ENTER OR RECEIVE A PRIZE

1. To enter the Sweepstakes and join the Reader Service, affix the Four Free Books and Free Gifts sticker along with both of your Sweepstakes stickers to the Sweepstakes Entry Form. If you do not wish to take advantage of our Reader Service, but wish to enter the Sweepstakes only, do not affix the Four Free Books and Free Gifts sticker; affix only the Sweepstakes stickers to the Sweepstakes Entry Form. Incomplete and/or inaccurate entries are ineligible for that section or sections of prizes. Torstar Corp. and its affiliates are not responsible for mutilated or unreadable entries or inadvertent printing errors. Mechanically reproduced entries are null and void.

2. Whether you take advantage of this offer or not, on or about April 30, 1992 at the offices of Marden-Kane Inc., Lake Success, NY, your Sweepstakes number will be compared against a list of winning numbers generated at random by the computer. However, prizes will only be awarded to individuals who have entered the Sweepstakes. In the event that all prizes are not claimed, a random drawing will be held from all qualified entries received from March 30, 1990 to March 31, 1992, to award all unclaimed prizes. All cash prizes (Grand to Sixth), will be mailed to the winners and are payable by check in U.S. funds. Seventh prize to be shipped to winners via third-class mail. These prizes are in addition to any free, surprise or mystery gifts that might be offered. Versions of this sweepstakes with different prizes of approximate equal value may appear in other mailings or at retail outlets by Torstar Corp. and its affiliates.

3. The following prizes are awarded in this sweepstakes: ★Grand Prize (1) $1,000,000; First Prize (1) $25,000; Second Prize (1) $10,000; Third Prize (5) $5,000; Fourth Prize (10) $1,000; Fifth Prize (100) $250; Sixth Prize (2,500) $10; ★★Seventh Prize (6,000) $12.95 ARV.

   ★This Sweepstakes contains a Grand Prize offering of a $1,000,000 annuity. Winner will receive $33,333.33 a year for 30 years without interest totalling $1,000,000.

   ★★Seventh Prize: A fully illustrated hardcover book published by Torstar Corp. Approximate Retail Value of the book is $12.95.

   Entrants may cancel the Reader Service at anytime without cost or obligation to buy (see details in center insert card).

4. Extra Bonus! This presentation offers two extra bonus prizes valued at a total of $33,000 to be awarded in a random drawing from all qualified entries received by March 31, 1992. No purchase necessary to enter or receive a prize. To qualify, see instructions on the insert card. Winner will have the choice of merchandise offered or a $33,000 check payable in U.S. funds. All other published rules and regulations apply.

5. This Sweepstakes is being conducted under the supervision of Marden-Kane, Inc., an independent judging organization. By entering this Sweepstakes, each entrant accepts and agrees to be bound by these rules and the decisions of the judges, which shall be final and binding. Odds of winning in the random drawing are dependent upon the total number of entries received. Taxes, if any, are the sole responsibility of the winners. Prizes are nontransferable. All entries must be received at the address printed on the reply card and must be postmarked no later than 12:00 MIDNIGHT on March 31, 1992. The drawing for all unclaimed Sweepstakes prizes and for the Bonus Sweepstakes Prize will take place May 30, 1992, at 12:00 NOON at the offices of Marden-Kane, Inc., Lake Success, NY.

6. This offer is open to residents of the U.S., the United Kingdom, France and Canada, 18 years or older, except employees and their immediate family members of Torstar Corp., its affiliates, subsidiaries, and all other agencies and persons connected with the use, marketing or conduct of this Sweepstakes. All Federal, State, Provincial and local laws apply. Void wherever prohibited or restricted by law. Any litigation within the Province of Quebec respecting the conduct and awarding of a prize in this publicity contest must be submitted to the Régie des Loteries et Courses du Québec.

7. Winners will be notified by mail and may be required to execute an affidavit of eligibility and release, which must be returned within 14 days after notification or an alternative winner will be selected. Canadian winners will be required to correctly answer an arithmetical skill-testing question administered by mail, which must be returned within a limited time. Winners consent to the use of their names, photographs and/or likenesses for advertising and publicity in conjunction with this and similar promotions without additional compensation.

8. For a list of our major winners, send a stamped, self-addressed envelope to: WINNERS LIST, c/o MARDEN-KANE, INC., P.O. BOX 701, SAYREVILLE, NJ 08871. Winners Lists will be fulfilled after the May 30, 1992 drawing date.

ALTERNATE MEANS OF ENTRY: Print your name and address on a 3″×5″ piece of plain paper and send to:

In the U.S.
Harlequin's WISHBOOK Sweepstakes
3010 Walden Ave.
P.O. Box 1867, Buffalo, NY 14269-1867

In Canada
Harlequin's WISHBOOK Sweepstakes
P.O. Box 609
Fort Erie, Ontario L2A 5X3

LTY-H491RRD

RELIVE THE MEMORIES....

All the way from turn-of-the-century Ellis Island to the future of the '90s...**A CENTURY OF AMERICAN ROMANCE** takes you on a nostalgic journey through the twentieth century.

Watch for all the **A CENTURY OF AMERICAN ROMANCE** titles coming to you one per month over the next two months in Harlequin American Romance, including #385 MY ONLY ONE by Eileen Nauman, in April.

Don't miss a day of **A CENTURY OF AMERICAN ROMANCE.**

The women . . . the men . . . the passions . . . the memories. . . .

If you missed #345 AMERICAN PIE, #349 SATURDAY'S CHILD, #353 THE GOLDEN RAINTREE, #357 THE SENSATION, #361 ANGELS WINGS, #365 SENTIMENTAL JOURNEY, #369 STRANGER IN PARADISE, #373 HEARTS AT RISK, or #377 TILL THE END OF TIME and would like to order them, send your name, address, and zip or postal code, along with a check or money order for $2.95 plus 75¢ postage and handling ($1.00 in Canada) *for each book ordered,* payable to Harlequin Reader Service, to:

In the U.S.
3010 Walden Ave.
Box 1325
Buffalo, NY 14269-1325

In Canada
P.O. Box 609
Fort Erie, Ontario
L2A 5X3

Please specify book title(s) with your order.
Canadian residents please add applicable federal and provincial taxes.

CA-80